**'Perhaps I'd**
**introduction**
**Dr Jameson.**
**my daughter.'**

Kate felt as if someone had reached out and tugged at her heart. So this was Nick's child. Pale and blonde-haired, so unlike him in looks, and yet, without a shadow of doubt, his.

He looked up, his gaze locking intently with Kate's for a few seconds before his mouth tightened and he returned his attention to the child.

Kate swallowed convulsively, feeling hot tears pricking suddenly beneath her lashes. Very solemnly she shook hands with the child. 'Hello, Ellie.'

'Hello, Dr Jameson,' came the shy response.

Kate smiled. 'It's lovely to meet you, Ellie, and, please, I'm sure we're going to be good friends, so why don't you call me Kate? That is…' she glanced up '…if your daddy doesn't mind?'

His gaze narrowed briefly. 'I don't see why not. If you're happy with that.'

**Jean Evans** was born in Leicester and married shortly before her seventeenth birthday. She has two married daughters and several grandchildren. She gains valuable information and background for her medical romances from her husband, who is a senior nursing administrator. She now lives in Hampshire, close to the New Forest and within easy reach of the historic city of Winchester.

**Recent titles by the same author:**

A LEAP IN THE DARK

# THE DEVOTED FATHER

## BY
## JEAN EVANS

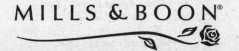

MILLS & BOON®

All the characters in this book have no existence outside the imagination of the author, and have no relation whatsoever to anyone bearing the same name or names. They are not even distantly inspired by any individual known or unknown to the author, and all the incidents are pure invention.

First published in Great Britain 2001
Harlequin Mills & Boon Limited,
Eton House, 18-24 Paradise Road, Richmond, Surrey TW9 1SR

© Jean Evans 2001

ISBN 0 263 82690 2

Set in Times Roman 10½ on 12 pt.
03-0901-48723

Printed and bound in Spain
by Litografia Rosés, S.A., Barcelona

# CHAPTER ONE

SOMETHING was wrong. Parking her car, Kate Jameson climbed out to stand on the gravel drive and stared at the small, stone-built cottage. It was in total darkness.

Shivering, she tugged the collar of her jacket together and rubbed her hands over her arms, feeling chilled in the night air which held the first hint of frost. A glance at her watch showed just after eight-thirty.

A slight smile curved her generous mouth as she reached into the car to retrieve her overnight bag and a suitcase before locking the door. Gramps had probably fallen asleep in front of his favourite TV programme, no doubt with a glass of his favourite whisky within easy reach.

Yes, that would be it. After all, he wouldn't have been expecting her for at least another hour. That was what she had told him when she had written a few days ago, but the traffic on the motorway from the south of England up to the small Derbyshire town had been sur- prisingly light.

Kate's hand shook slightly as she inserted her key in the lock and let herself in only to experience a new feel- ing of anxiety as she stepped on an assortment of en- velopes lying scattered on the mat. Her gaze swept the narrow hallway. It was cold—too cold—and there was a faint smell of damp. She shivered. Perhaps the ancient heating boiler had finally given up the ghost.

Setting her bags down, Kate tugged off her gloves and

bent to gather up the mail before making her way towards the sitting room.

'Gramps, I'm home. Surprise!'

Grinning, she pushed open the door and came to a halt. The room was in darkness. 'Gramps?' Her hand fumbled for the light switch, flipped it on, off, on again. Nothing happened. Frowning she moved towards the large open fireplace. As her eyes adjusted to the moonlight she could see evidence of a fire having been lit but the embers were cold.

Turning slowly, Kate surveyed the room's comfortable, if slightly old-fashioned furnishings. Nothing seemed out of place. Everything had been left neat and tidy. So why was a feeling of panic beginning to set in?

'Gramps?' Her breath fanned white into the air. Dropping the bundle of mail onto the coffee-table, she hurried towards the stairs. Again she reached for the light switch—again nothing happened. With a tiny sigh of annoyance she made her way slowly, up the stairs. But it was the same story there. The bed was neatly made and yet she sensed that something was wrong.

Kate felt her throat tighten. 'Now, don't start letting your imagination run away with you,' she muttered under her breath. 'What could possibly be wrong?' If there had been a burglary there would be some evidence. Things scattered around, a broken window. No, there had to be a perfectly logical explanation. Maybe Gramps had unexpectedly had to go out. She gave a slight laugh. There would be a note somewhere. In the kitchen, propped against the teapot where they always used to leave messages for each other. Yes, that would be it. Reassured, her steps quickened. Her heels clicked on the stairs as she edged her way carefully down, and then she heard something.

A muffled sound suddenly disturbed the silence. A door closed. Someone—something—was moving about. Kate froze. There was someone else in the cottage. A burglar, or worse! She peered down into the darkness, her heart pounding as a shadowy figure appeared in the glow of the moonlight from the half-open sitting-room doorway.

Kate's breath snagged in her throat. She watched, tensing as a door closed and the man moved into the hallway. Maybe if she didn't move, didn't make a sound, he might pass her by.

But he didn't. Suddenly he was staring straight at her, moonlight throwing the hard planes and angles of his features into harsh focus.

Easing a stray wisp of chestnut hair from her eyes, Kate stared down at the intruder. He was tall, around six feet, that much she could judge even from her precarious stance.

The eyes, she discovered, belonged to a ruggedly chiselled face. His hair was dark, and there was a hint of designer stubble on his chin.

He looked, at the same time, faintly disreputable and dangerously male, and his uninvited presence in the cottage was having a thoroughly unsettling effect on her.

His eyes narrowed, shifting over her with cool, unhurried precision.

'You must be Kate,' he said, and his voice was deep and gritty, sending an odd sensation tingling along her nerve-endings. 'I've been expecting you.'

Kate had never met this man before in her life, yet somehow she sensed that escape was not going to be an option. She huddled, half-crouched on the stairs, and looked down at him. 'Who...who are you? How did you get in?'

Powerful shoulders moved beneath a black sweatshirt. 'Don't you think you'd be more comfortable if you came down to ground level? Here, let me help.'

He moved towards her and held out a hand. Kate half rose, taking an uncertain step back up the stairs. In the process the heel of her shoe became snagged in the hem of her skirt. She gave a brief cry of alarm, swayed and, instinctively it seemed, he reached out, grasping her arms, drawing her slowly towards him.

Her hands encountered his chest and for several seconds it seemed she was held within the circle of his arms. Colour flared in her cheeks as his eyes glinted briefly with humour.

'There you are, perfectly safe.' He released her and she edged back unsteadily, suddenly conscious, as he moved into a pale circle of moonlight, of every line of his tall frame, from his shoulders beneath the sweatshirt to a slim waist and lean thighs beneath the faded jeans he was wearing.

There was something compelling about his tanned features, along with something else, something vaguely unsettling.

Kate faced him, breathing hard. 'Perhaps you'd be good enough to tell me what you're doing here. I don't know you. Or perhaps you make a habit of invading other people's privacy?'

His gaze narrowed briefly. 'The name is Forrester. Nick Forrester.' He proffered his hand. 'This isn't exactly the way I'd planned things. I live close by so Alec asked me to—'

Kate cut him off sharply. 'You know Gramps?'

'For quite some time.' He gave a wry smile. 'I joined the practice here in Felldale about eighteen months ago.'

Kate frowned. 'I don't understand. So, where *is*

Gramps? Why isn't he here?' She gave a slight laugh. 'Don't tell me, he's forgotten I was coming. I know he's been a bit out of sorts lately, not to mention slightly forgetful. He didn't even answer my last letter—'

'Look, I think you'd better sit down.'

'I don't want to sit down.' Panic suddenly gave an edge to her voice. 'Something's wrong, I know it is. Gramps would be here.'

'Look, there's no easy way to say this. I wish there was.' He raked a hand through his hair. 'I'm afraid it's a bit more serious than a bit out of sorts. Your grandfather is in hospital. That's really why I'm here. I came in to collect a few things for him, and to see if you'd arrived. He glanced round the semi-dark hallway. 'I'm afraid we've had another damn power cut.'

Kate felt as if her breath was suddenly stuck in her lungs, needing a desperate effort to drive it upwards. 'What…what happened to Gramps?'

'He had a heart attack, a couple of days ago.' He seemed to anticipate her next question. 'It was pretty bad but he was taken straight to the coronary care unit. I can promise you, he's in very good hands—the best.'

Kate heard her own voice sounding strangely calm and wondered how it was possible when her brain was in a state of turmoil. 'How is he?'

'He's stable now that they've managed to control the pain. Obviously, it's early days…'

She looked at him and gave a harsh laugh. 'Spare me the platitudes, Dr Forrester. I'm not one of your patients. I'm a doctor and this is my grandfather we're talking about.'

He glanced at her stricken face and nodded. 'You're right. I didn't mean to sound patronising but right now it's probably the only information anyone can give you.

It is early days. As I said, the pain is being controlled. Everything that can be done is being done.'

'But why wasn't I told? Why didn't you—*someone*—let me know?'

'Alec didn't want you to worry. He kept insisting it was indigestion. You know how stubborn he can be? I did manage to find your phone number and I tried to call you but I couldn't get any reply. I'm sorry. I did try.'

'No.' Kate closed her eyes briefly and shook her head. 'It isn't your fault. You did what you could. I left a couple of days earlier than I'd planned so that I could call and see a friend on the way here.' She drew a deep breath and straightened up. 'I have to go and see him.'

'It's getting late.'

'I don't care. I want to see him. I'd never forgive myself if...' Her voice broke. She fumbled in her bag. 'My car keys. I put them down somewhere.'

'We'll take my car.'

'There's really no need.'

Nick Forrester's mouth tightened. 'I'd say there is. You're tired. You've already driven a long way and you're in a state of shock.'

He was already ahead of her, ushering her into the cold night air, opening the car door. 'Just get in.'

The softly spoken words brought her back to reality and she found herself moving instinctively, her actions becoming automatic. He was right. She *was* tired. More than that, she suddenly felt exhausted. The past few months hadn't exactly been easy and now this, just when she had thought she was beginning to get her life back together again.

It was almost a relief to do as she was told, to let this total stranger take control. She let her head fall back against the seat and closed her eyes thinking, Please, don't die, Gramps. You musn't die. Without even being aware of it she gave a deep sigh.

Nick took his eyes briefly from the road. 'Bear up, Kate. He's going to need you.'

She nodded, her throat so tight that speech hurt. 'I'll never forgive myself for not being here.'

'Hey, come on. You weren't to know Alec was going to have a heart attack.'

But it was no excuse. In the past Gramps had always been there for her when she had needed him, and now, when the situation was reversed, she had let him down.

They reached the hospital and Kate climbed, shivering, out of the car. She was vaguely aware of Nick's hand beneath her arm, preventing her from stumbling, as if he sensed that without it she would have fallen.

They hurried towards the hospital building and made their way through Reception. He was beside her as they walked the seemingly endless length of the corridors. Doors opened beneath the firm pressure of his hand and he guided her through.

She shot him a glance. 'You don't have to do this, you know. I can manage.'

'I want to,' he insisted quietly. 'I'm concerned for Alec, too.'

She didn't argue. Despite the fact that he was a stranger, right now she just knew that she was glad to have him there, taking charge.

'I'd better make some enquiries first.' Nick led her gently to one of the chairs in a waiting area.

'But—'

'I know how much you want to see him, Kate, but it is late.' He glanced at his watch. 'Night staff will have come on duty. They may still be doing the report. I have to check with them first, out of courtesy.'

She knew he was right. He brought her coffee in a plastic cup. It was hot and too strong but she drank it anyway. Doors opened and swung soundlessly to closed. Her heart gave a thud each time a nurse appeared, only to smile and bustle away.

Nick came back minutes later and Kate rose unsteadily to her feet. She found herself desperately searching his face.

'I've spoken to Sister. There's been no significant change in his condition, which is probably about as good as we can hope for right now. We can see him for a few minutes but, remember, he needs to rest.'

He led her into a small room where a nurse was checking monitors. Kate stared at the frail figure in the bed, surrounded by wires and tubes. She had seen it all before so many times, this working paraphernalia of a busy hospital, but somehow it was different when it was Gramps lying there with his eyes closed, the oxygen mask over his nose and mouth. Suddenly he looked older and smaller and very vulnerable.

Sister June Beckett, tall, dark-haired and attractive in her blue uniform, smiled briefly. 'Dr Forrester. And it's Dr Jameson, isn't it?'

Kate nodded. 'How is he?'

'He's relaxed since we managed to control the pain.' Sister returned a clipboard to its place at the foot of the bed and smiled wryly. 'Unfortunately, doctors never make the best patients. They know all the answers but seem to assume that they only apply to other people. Isn't that right, Dr Jameson?' She reached out, her fingers gently feeling for his pulse and looking at her fob watch. Alec Jameson's eyes fluttered open. 'Well, that's not too bad. You have a visitor.' She smiled at Kate. 'You won't stay too long, will you? We don't want him getting overtired.'

'We'll only stay for a couple of minutes.' It was Nick who gave the reassurance.

'Well, in that case— Oh, no, there's the phone again. No peace for the wicked.' Her slim figure sped away.

Kate looked down at the frail figure lying propped up against his pillows. Nick stood aside, allowing her to move closer. She swallowed hard.

'Gramps. Oh, Gramps, what have you been doing to yourself?'

'Kate, my dear, this is a nice surprise.' His hand fluttered to the oxygen mask.

'How are you feeling?'

'Oh, a bit sleepy, but they tell me that's to be expected.'

'You're not in pain?'

'No, not any more.' He gave a slight smile. 'Don't let all this gadgetry fool you. I'm fine—really.'

She reached out to clasp his hand. 'Gramps, why didn't you tell me you were ill?' she chided gently.

'Because there was nothing to tell. Thought it was the damned indigestion, only this time the pain didn't go away.' He glanced up at Nick. 'If it hadn't been for this young man, things might have been very different. He found me, got me to the hospital.' He laughed wheezily. 'The rest, I'm pleased to say, is all a bit of a blur.'

Alec patted his granddaughter's hand. 'You're not to worry about me, my dear. Seeing you is the best tonic I could have wished for, and I'm doing just fine.'

Kate wished she could believe it, but she wasn't fooled. The change in Gramps had shocked her, even though she was careful not to let it show. There was a greyish tinge about his lips which told its own story.

Her throat tightened. She lifted his hand, pressing it to her cheek. 'We can't stay for long. Sister says you need to rest, and she's right.'

His grey eyes twinkled. 'She's a bossy young woman and I told her so.' For a moment the smiled faded. 'They keep taking my temperature, giving me pills to swallow. Never a minute's peace.'

'They're doing their job.' Kate smiled.

'I know. But you know I hate fuss.'

'Yes, I do, but it's for your own good. Let them help you, Gramps. That way you'll get out of here so much quicker.' She leaned forward to refill a glass with water from a jug on the bedside locker. 'Try to rest and relax and just concentrate on getting well.'

'I'm worried about the practice, Kate. Nick and Huw are both first-class doctors, but it isn't fair they should shoulder the whole burden, especially at this time of year.'

'I'm sure they're doing just fine, Gramps.' She glanced over her shoulder at Nick, who smiled.

'Of course we are, Alec. Kate's right, you should concentrate on getting well. Huw and I can cope with the odd extra night call.'

'There, you see? So no excuses.'

Alec gave a tired smile which didn't quite reach his eyes. 'I've tried to persuade Nick that we need a locum, if only to ease my conscience, just until I'm back on my feet again.'

Kate's gaze flickered in Nick's direction but he was already ahead of her.

'I'm looking into it, Alec. Don't worry, I'll keep you in the picture.'

Alec nodded and closed his eyes briefly before opening them again. 'It's lovely to see you again, Kate, my dear. How long can you stay?'

She patted his hand. 'I'm not going anywhere, Gramps, at least not until I've seen you back on your feet again.'

'You don't have to do this, my dear—'

'It's all right, Gramps. I've completed my contract and I've left my options open. I don't have to make any decisions for a while.' She looked up as Sister entered the room.

'Time's up, I'm afraid. Here we are, Dr Jameson. I've brought you a nice cup of cocoa. Drink up and then we'll settle you down for the night.'

'See what a dragon she is?' He gave a throaty chuckle. 'Rules with a rod of iron.'

'Give some people an inch and they'll take a mile,' June Beckett said with mock severity as she set the cup down on the bedside cabinet and shook down a thermometer before popping it into his mouth.

'I'll see you tomorrow, Gramps.' Kate bent to kiss him. His eyes were closed. He was already half-asleep.

'Come on,' Nick prompted gently. 'There's nothing more you can do tonight.'

'I hate to leave him.'

'I know, but what he needs now is to sleep, and time for the medication to work. He'll need you to be strong and you'll do that best if you're not dead on your feet.'

She knew it made sense but it didn't make it any easier to walk away. A wave of exhaustion hit her again as they made their way out to the car and she was glad Nick didn't attempt to make any conversation as they drove back. Too many thoughts were spinning round in her head.

Back at the cottage she climbed wearily out of the car. It was a dark, clear night and the temperature had dropped several more degrees in the past hour. She shivered.

'Come on, let's get you inside.'

'I'll be fine, really.' She looked at him. 'You've been very kind. I...I don't know how to thank you.'

'Don't even think about it.' He took the key from her and opened the door. He flipped the light switch. 'Well, at least they've managed to get the power back on. How about a cup of coffee? I think we could both use one, don't you?'

A complete stranger was taking charge and she was only too happy to go along with it. Before she knew what was happening she was ensconced at the table with a steaming mug of coffee in front of her. 'Mmm, that's good. I hadn't realised how cold I was.'

'That's natural. You're still suffering from shock.' He moved to the kitchen fire, struck a match and lit the kindling which had been laid ready. He watched it for a few seconds as it began to burn. 'This should help to warm the place up a bit.'

Nick's gaze narrowed as he studied Kate's appearance, seeing the dark shadows beneath her eyes. His gaze roamed from the soft tumble of her hair to the generous curve of her mouth. 'You don't look old enough to be a doctor.'

'I'm twenty-seven,' she snapped defensively.

He gave a slight smile. 'It's not exactly been the best of homecomings, has it?'

She certainly couldn't disagree with that. Her thoughts were in turmoil as she struggled to imagine the practice without Gramps. It didn't bear thinking on. He had been there for as long as she could remember, a stable anchor in her life. Her fingers tightened shakily on the mug.

'He looked so ill.' Her throat tightened. 'He was always such an active man.'

'He still is.' Nick frowned. 'You've got to start thinking positively. Alec is a fighter and we both know how much a positive attitude counts in a situation like this.'

Kate smoothed a finger round the rim of the mug and glanced up at him. 'He must have been ill for some time. I can't believe I didn't know what was happening, that I didn't get some hint from his letters. I mean, I thought there was something, but when I mentioned it he just said he'd been a bit out of sorts.'

Nick drained his coffee and set the mug down. 'Alec didn't want you to know. He wanted you to get on with your own life. It was important to him.'

Blue eyes slanted in Kate's direction and she tried to tell herself that she had imagined the note of censure in his voice.

She expelled a harsh breath. 'I had my reasons for leaving Felldale.' Draining the dregs of her own coffee, Kate pushed the mug away and rose to her feet. She certainly wasn't about to share those reasons with this man.

'I'm sure you did. I wasn't making a judgement. I'm just saying that Alec often talked about you. He missed you.'

Nick Forrester was tall and slim and once again she was immediately conscious of every line of his body, from the taut shoulders to the slender waist and lean thighs beneath the jeans he was wearing.

With a determined effort, she dragged her gaze up to meet his, saying briskly, 'You said you joined the practice about eighteen months ago. I remember now, in one of his letters, Gramps mentioned that you were a consultant at the local hospital.'

'Yes, that's right.'

'So why would you leave that to become a GP in a small place like Felldale?' She shot him a glance and felt her throat tighten for a few seconds as she became aware of the shrewd blue eyes meeting hers.

'It suited my purpose. There were a few personal problems I needed to sort out. I'd got to know Alec quite well through referrals of patients to my clinic.' He frowned. 'I gather he took on a locum for a while, then I heard he was looking for someone on a more permanent basis.' He shrugged. 'As I said, I needed a change of direction. It all seemed to come together at the right time, for both of us.'

Kate collected the mugs and put them into the sink. She bit at her lower lip. 'Look, I...I meant what I said. I really appreciate what you've done. It can't have been easy, covering Gramps's surgeries as well as your own.'

'We've coped.'

'But there's a limit to how long you can go on carrying the extra workload.' Kate frowned. 'Gramps is right. You need a locum, if only to put his mind at rest.'

He gave a slight laugh. 'The only flaw in the argument is that doctors aren't exactly flocking to the area. In case you've forgotten, Felldale is a little off the beaten track and the onset of winter isn't likely to add to its attractions. Even if we could find someone willing to join us, I don't know how long the situation is likely to last. It's early days. There's no way of knowing how long Alec's recovery will take.'

'So what's going to happen to the practice?'

He gave a crooked smile. 'Isn't that rather up to you?'

'Me?' She stared at him. 'I don't understand.'

'You must know that Alec always hoped that some day you'd join him at the practice on a permanent basis? I gather you'd previously done some locum work for him.'

Kate stared at him. 'I had no idea. Gramps never mentioned it.'

'Maybe he hoped it would come from you. But I dare say you have other plans.'

Her throat tightened. 'I've had an offer, but they don't need an answer for a while yet.' She looked at him. 'What exactly are you suggesting?'

He frowned. 'Would it really be so difficult for you to stay on in Felldale for a while? You have no definite plans, you know the area. I'd guess you know most of the local people.'

'So, what…? You're suggesting that I should join the practice?'

Nick's mouth twisted. 'It seems a good idea to me, and you don't need me to tell you how much it would mean to Alec. It would certainly put his mind at rest.' He frowned. 'The simple truth is that, yes, Huw and I can keep things going for a while, but sooner or later things will begin to suffer. I'm sure I don't need to spell out what can happen if an emergency call comes through at the wrong time. If neither of us can deal with it because we're with other patients.' He looked at her. 'I'd assumed you'd want to stay around Felldale at least long enough to see Alec back on his feet.'

'Yes, of course.'

'So, what's the problem? I mean it, Kate. We could use you.'

She moistened her dry lips with her tongue, feeling the familiar sense of panic welling up inside her. Coming back to Felldale hadn't been part of her plans. A fleeting visit, no more. 'It isn't that simple.'

'Things never are.' There was a note of cynicism in his voice and she gave a sigh of exasperation.

'You don't understand. Look, I'm sure you'll find someone else.'

'I don't doubt it.' His voice hardened. 'But it will take time and that's the one thing we don't have. You've seen the effect all of this is having on Alec. We need help *now*. I don't want to have to wait until a patient's life is in jeopardy because we're overstretched and can't get to them in time.'

His mouth twisted. 'I'm not looking for a lifetime's commitment, Dr Jameson, just a few weeks of your precious time.' His blue eyes became glittering slits. 'But, of course, I was forgetting, you have other, more urgent commitments. You don't feel any sense of responsibility towards anyone but yourself, do you, Doctor? It's far easier to opt out, isn't it?'

Kate almost choked. The man was insufferable. 'That's unfair.'

'Is it?' His mouth tightened briefly.

'You don't understand.'

'Try me.'

'I…' She eased a stray wisp of hair behind her ear in a nervous gesture.

'As I see it, we both want the same thing—for Alec to get well. He's not going to do that if he's lying in his hospital bed, fretting about what's going on here. Don't you owe him, Doctor? He needs peace of mind. Is it too much to ask?'

He made it all sound so simple. She had spent the past two years putting as much distance as she could between herself and memories that had been raw and painful. He didn't…couldn't possibly know what he was asking.

But, then, maybe he was right, the thought came homing in. She did owe it to Gramps, because she loved him and because he'd had no choice when her parents had been killed in a car crash all those years ago, mown down by a lorry driver who had fallen asleep at the wheel. But he had taken her in and raised her.

And more than that—Kate's chin rose—maybe she owed it to herself to put the past finally where it belonged—behind her.

As if aware of the silent battle going on inside her, Nick took a step towards her and offered his hand. 'So, what do you say? Do we have a deal?'

For a moment she stared at him, her glance flicking up to meet his narrowed blue gaze as she hesitated before slowly advancing her own fingers nervously towards him.

'I'd like to think we can be friends, Kate. Is that too much to ask? Don't you think we could give it a try?'

Friends! Somehow she felt it wasn't a word she would ever be able to apply to her feelings about Nick Forrester. She drew a deep breath. How did you deal with an unknown quantity?

Almost as if he'd read her thoughts, he frowned and said softly, 'Is it really so difficult?' He met her anxious eyes and said softly, 'You won't regret it.'

She wanted to believe him, but it wasn't easy when part of her was already regretting it.

He held out his hand. Kate slid hers into it. It felt strong and warm.

'Yes, all right, we have a deal. I'll stay, for as long as Gramps needs me.'

It was only later that she began to think seriously

about what she had let herself in for. She didn't know anything about Nick, except that he seemed to have the ability to provoke a great many emotions in her, none of which was going to make for an easy working relationship. But, then, she told herself firmly, it *was* only a temporary arrangement, until Gramps was better, not for a lifetime. Surely she could survive that?

# CHAPTER TWO

'YOU might notice a few changes since you were last here.' Smiling, Practice Manager Jill Stewart led Kate through to the small office. 'You'll be pleased to see that the dreaded shelves have been replaced, and we've updated the computer system just for a start.'

Kate eyed the latest state-of-the-art equipment and grinned. 'What? You mean Gramps actually agreed to give up on the old card filing system at long last?'

Jill grinned. 'Ah, well, I won't say it happened overnight and not without a certain amount of resistance.'

'I can believe it.'

'But in the end I think even Alec had to admit that we couldn't go on as we were. I mean, apart from anything else, we were running out of shelf space so, when it came to a choice between building an extension to the surgery or bringing in the computers, I think it was probably the lesser of two evils as far as he was concerned.'

'Poor Gramps.' Kate smiled. 'It isn't that he disapproves of modern technology, he just finds it very difficult to come to terms with it all.'

Jill chuckled. 'On a bad day I'm not too keen on it myself.'

'I still can't imagine how you managed to persuade him.'

Jill gathered up a bundle of mail, flipped through it and dropped it onto the desk. 'Ah, well, we have Nick to thank for that. He can be very persuasive, can our Nick.'

Kate could believe it! A couple of hours in Nick Forrester's company had been more than enough to persuade her that he knew exactly how to get what he wanted—and that he would resort to almost any means to get it. She blinked hard in a determined effort to shut out a thoroughly disturbing image of his face and was glad when they made their way through to Reception.

'Nothing much in the way of changes here, I'm glad to say. We thought you might like to use Alec's consulting room. Huw Roberts isn't in yet, but he's due any time. He uses the room at the end of the corridor. But, of course, you already know that. And Dr Forrester is next to the treatment room. You'll remember Annie, I'm sure.'

'Hi.' Replacing the phone, Annie Davies scribbled a note before she looked up and grinned. 'It's great to see you back. Dr Forrester said you'd be in some time. We didn't expect you till later on your first day, but I'm certainly glad to see you.' Smiling, Annie ruefully indicated the pile of patients' case notes. 'I'm afraid you're going to be thrown in at the deep end.'

'Oh, well.' Kate smiled wryly. 'That's what I'm here for. Might as well start the way we mean to go on.' She leaned over the desk to peer at the morning's appointment list. 'From the look of things it might be a good idea if I were to get started.'

'Uh-oh. Here we go again.' Annie reached for the phone, adding yet another name to the list as she spoke into it. 'Yes, Mrs Stevens, that will be fine. You bring young Harry along to the surgery. You may have to wait a while, but Doctor will see you as soon as she can.'

Jill handed Kate a bundle of cards and nodded ruefully in the direction of the waiting room. 'It's worse than usual because of the chicken pox, I'm afraid. We have an epidemic on our hands. The kiddies from the local school are going down like flies.'

'Oh, great!' Kate grinned. 'Still, I suppose forewarned is forearmed. I suppose Dr Forrester has already made a start?'

'He sometimes manages to get in early. He likes to take advantage of a quiet spell to catch up on some of his letters—that sort of thing.'

'Kate! Kate Jameson. It *is* you.'

At the sound of the familiar voice coming from behind her, Kate turned and laughed as she was suddenly caught up in a bear-like hug.

'Huw!'

Brown eyes twinkled as Huw Roberts held her briefly at arm's length before hugging her again. Forty years old, of medium height and good-looking, he finally set her free to clasp her hand in a warm, firm grip.

'I heard you were back.' His voice bore a heavy trace of a Welsh accent. 'I'm only sorry it had to be under such circumstances, *cariad*. But one thing you have to say for Alec, he's a fighter.'

She gave a tight smile. 'Yes, he is.'

'So, you've come back to us, then.'

'Temporarily, Huw,' she cautioned. 'I'm helping out, that's all.'

'Aye, well, I'm delighted.' He held her at arm's length again, briefly scanning her pale face. 'We've about two years of gossip to catch up on, girl.' He looked at his watch and pulled a face. 'Perhaps we'll get a chance to talk later.'

'I shall look forward to it.' Kate smiled, feeling some of her nervousness ebb away. Coming home might not be so bad after all, she thought as she made her way to the consulting room, taking a few seconds to run a comb through her hair before pressing the bell to summon her first patient.

Her gaze travelled critically over the bronze-coloured silk shirt and the knee-length skirt. Moving to sit at the desk, she pressed the bell, switched on the computer and watched it flicker into life as she waited.

Andrew Hopkins was new to the area. He was thirty-five years old, worked with computers and confessed to being something of a keep-fit fanatic, so it came as a surprise to see him sitting opposite her looking pale and less than happy.

'I'm going deaf,' he said without preamble. 'I had a cold a couple of weeks ago.' He held his hand up to the left side of his head. 'I noticed then that everything sounded a bit muffled.' He gave a slight smile. 'I thought at first everyone had suddenly started talking in whispers. You know, as a joke. I wouldn't have put it past the crowd I work with. Then, gradually, I realised it wasn't a joke. It was me.'

'Is it just the one ear that's affected or both?'

'Just the one. This side is fine.'

'And can you hear anything at all with the bad ear?'

'A sort of ringing noise. It's a nuisance. I just can't get away from it. Nothing makes it go away and it's really starting to get me down.'

'Yes, I can imagine.' Kate was on her feet, reaching for her auriscope. 'Have you had any earache, any pain at all in that ear?'

'Well, now that you mention it, it was bothering me a bit last week. I got this sudden stabbing pain and it's been giving me trouble ever since.'

'Let's take a quick look and see if we can see what's going on. I'll try not to hurt you.' Kate made her examination, checking both ears as gently as possible. Even so, Andrew Hopkins flinched. 'Sorry about that.' She straightened. 'Well, the right ear is fine. A bit pink but nothing to worry about. The left ear looks quite nasty, though. I'm not surprised it's painful or that you can't hear properly.'

Seating herself at the desk again, she brought up the patient's previous history on the computer screen. 'Have you noticed any bleeding or discharge from the ear?'

'Well, yes, slightly. I've been feeling a bit dizzy, too.'

'Mr Hopkins, why didn't you come to the surgery before this?'

He looked slightly sheepish. 'Oh, you know how it is. Busy at work. Don't want to be a wimp.' He pulled a face. 'Tell you the truth, I was a bit scared, too. My dad went deaf. We didn't really notice it too much at first, it happened so gradually.' He looked at Kate. 'I suppose I thought it was happening to me as well and all I could think was, well, that's the job and everything else going down the drain.'

Kate gave an exasperated smile. 'Someone could have put your mind at rest if you'd come to the surgery. You could have had a chat with Sue, our nurse. She's on duty most days. As it is, you have a nasty ear infection. I'll give you some antibiotics which should clear it, and you can take some painkillers, something like paracetamol if you feel you need something for the pain.' She tapped in a prescription, printed it out, signed it and rose to her feet. Andrew Hopkins followed suit.

'Thanks, Doc.'

'No problem. Just don't blow your nose too hard and no swimming for a while. Make sure you complete the course of antibiotics, and if things don't seem any better, come and see me again.'

'Will do.'

He went on his way and Kate returned to her desk.

It was a busy but satisfying morning, during which she saw a steady stream of patients. Inevitably she saw several red-eyed children, obviously all in the first stages of chicken pox. There was the usual spate of coughs, sore throats and backache.

Kate pressed the bell summoning her next patient. Tall and wiry, Mabel Carter was fifty years old but looked more as she settled herself into the chair. Kate smiled and briefly scanned her computer notes. 'Hello, Mrs Carter. The usual blood-pressure check, is it?' She reached for the cuff, winding it gently round the woman's upper arm before reaching for her stethoscope.

'And how is old Dr Jameson, my dear? I was sorry to hear he was so poorly. It must have been a bit of a shock for you.'

Kate had answered the same question, with slight variations, at least ten times that morning, but, knowing that it reflected a touching and very genuine concern, she swallowed hard and said, 'Yes, it was, rather.' She straightened up, removed the cuff and made a note, before looking up.

'I heard it was a heart attack.'

'Yes, that's right. But the hospital seems to be pleased with his progress.'

'Aye, well, I'm glad to hear it. You know my feelings about hospitals.'

Kate looked at the older woman and smiled. 'How are things, then, Mabel? It's been a while since I last popped over to the farm to see you.'

'Oh, nowt changes much. Dad's pretty much the same. Some days are better than others but I suppose that's the way it goes.' She sighed as she rolled her sleeve down. 'He's gone downhill this past six months. He can't dress himself any more, not without help, and that doesn't please him.'

Kate nodded sympathetically. Bert Carter was nearly eighty years old and had been diagnosed three years ago as having Alzheimer's disease. 'Would you like me to come and see him one day fairly soon, Mabel? Just to check him over.'

'You'll not get any sense out of him,' Mabel said with brisk resignation. 'He'll talk to you fine one minute and forget all about it two minutes later.'

'Yes, I'm afraid that's one of the classic symptoms of the disease. It must be very distressing for you.'

'I cope. Not much point railing against it, is there? He's my dad, my responsibility.'

Kate had long since learned not to expect any other answer. She sat back in her chair. 'It's you I'm really worried about, Mabel,' she said gently. 'What about *your* health? Nursing someone, especially someone close to you, who has Alzheimer's is exhausting and some-times a soul-destroying job, no matter how much you love them.'

For a few seconds, Mabel's eyes were suspiciously bright. She blinked hard. An only child, brought up on a farm which had, until a few years ago been run by her father, Mabel had grown up tough, knowing that she was depended upon to give a hand.

Rumour had it that there had been one serious love in Mabel's life. It hadn't survived her parents' need of her and she had never contemplated marriage since.

Gradually, after her mother's death and her father's deteriorating health, Mabel had taken over the running of the farm. The results were painfully obvious, but

Mabel had never been a quitter and she wasn't about to start now.

'You can see him if you feel you must,' she said, gathering up her bags. 'It won't do no good. There's nothing to be done, we both know that. He doesn't even know who I am these days…' Her voice trailed away.

Kate bit at her lower lip. 'We could try again, to find a place—'

'No.' Mabel rose decisively to her feet. 'I know you mean it for the best, Doctor, and don't think it's not much appreciated. But I can manage. He's flesh and blood and I'll look after him as long as I can.'

Kate smiled gently, signed a prescription and rose to her feet. 'This is for your usual tablets, Mabel.' She looked at the woman's pale, drawn features. 'You know where I am if you need me. If you change your mind.'

'I won't, but I thank you for the thought, Doctor.'

Kate held back a sigh as the woman made her way out. It was one of the most frustrating aspects of the job, Kate decided, something she had never quite managed to come to terms with—the patient who refused help, whether out of fear or, as in Mabel Carter's case, misplaced pride.

She was still thinking about it five minutes later when she made her way along the corridor to Reception where she deposited the bundle of case notes on the desk before heading towards the small staffroom.

The waiting room was empty at last and the phones had finally stopped ringing, so she experienced a tiny flutter of surprise, having imagined she would be alone, to find Nick there, helping himself to coffee.

He had removed his jacket to reveal a blue shirt. He looked thinner than she had imagined. Thinner and tired.

He looked up as she hesitated in the doorway. 'I had a feeling you'd be along soon. Coffee?'

'Mmm, yes, please. Black, two sugars.'

He handed her the cup. 'So, how did it go?'

She gave a wry smile. 'The patients all wanted to know how Alec is, so by the time I'd given each one of them a progress report everything took twice as long as it should have done.' She gave a slight laugh. 'Apart from that, I think I managed to get through without too many mishaps.' She frowned. 'I saw Mabel Carter.'

'Ah.'

'You know her?'

'I've been out to the farm on a couple of occasions, when her father was ill.' He threw her a glance which scanned her taut expression. 'You won't be able to help her. Mabel doesn't want help. There's no point in blaming yourself. You simply have to learn to accept it.'

'It's not that easy.'

Nick gave a crooked smile. 'No, and it doesn't get any easier, does it? In spite of what they say.' He set his cup down, looked at his watch and frowned. 'Time I wasn't here. I'm hoping to see old Jim Pearson this afternoon. As a matter of fact, I was rather hoping you'd go with me.'

Kate's hand jerked spasmodically, spilling coffee into the saucer. 'You want *me* to come with you? To see a patient?'

'I'd be grateful.' He dropped the case notes into his briefcase, snapping the locks before reaching for his jacket. 'The truth is, I'll be glad of some moral support.' He frowned. 'You must know Jim? He's another character who's a bit too stubborn for his own good. A bit like Mabel Carter, except that Jim won't even acknowledge that he has a problem.'

Kate smiled. 'Nothing changes there, then? Although I must say, he seemed to be coping pretty well last time I saw him.'

'Which was how long ago?'

'Well, I suppose, now that you mention it, probably two years ago.'

Nick nodded. 'I think you'll find things have changed a bit since then.'

'In what way?'

'Basically, he's not looking after himself.' Nick ran a hand through his dark hair. 'His wife died about three years ago.'

'Yes, I remember. It hit him pretty hard. He and Ethel had been together a long time.'

'The problem is, I think she was what kept him going. His arthritis has been getting steadily worse. He's on the list for a hip replacement. His knee is in a pretty poor state, too, and I gather, from a neighbour, that he's had a bit of a fall. I know he's in pain.'

'And obviously you've tried him on anti-inflammatories?'

'Obviously. The problem is that he can't tolerate them and as a result he's more or less confined to his bed. On a good day he can get himself into a chair. On a bad day, even with the help of a neighbour or the district nurse, it's too painful for him.'

Kate frowned. 'I take it he gets help with meals, cleaning, that sort of thing?'

'As much as he'll accept. Like I said, he's as stubborn as they come and he never complains.'

'That sounds like Jim.' She looked at him. 'So what do you want me to do?'

'Ideally I'd like to see him move in with a relative

who can give him the care he needs, but he won't even consider the idea.'

'There's a daughter, isn't there?'

'So I gather.'

'And would she be prepared to take him on, even supposing you could persuade Jim?'

'She says so.' He frowned. 'Which leaves only one alternative. Residential care obviously wouldn't work. He needs medical care.'

'So you're talking about a nursing home.' Kate gave a slight laugh. 'I don't give much for your chances. Maybe he's happier where he is, despite everything.'

'Maybe,' he acknowledged. 'I'm all for allowing an elderly, possibly infirm person their independence but, as a doctor, I still have a duty of care. Where do you draw the line?'

'I don't know. I'm glad it's not my decision.' Kate looked at him. 'I'm still not sure what you think I can do.'

'You can give me an objective assessment, a second opinion, and, if necessary, your support, when—*if*—it comes to trying to persuade Jim that we're acting in his best interests.' He looked at her. 'Will you come?'

Kate studied him unhappily then nodded. 'Yes, all right, I'll come. Just as long as it's understood that I'm doing this against my better judgement.'

'Understood.' He gave a faint smile. 'We'll take my car.'

'Yes, fine. Just give me a couple of minutes to collect my things and I'll be with you.'

It was raining five minutes later when she hurried across the car park and slid into the passenger seat beside Nick. As they headed along the narrow, curving roads she studied him unhappily.

'I'm still not convinced I can do anything to help,' she warned. 'I know Jim Pearson can be stubborn. He may be elderly and frail, but if he decides he wants to stay where he is I won't stand by and see him bullied.'

A spasm flickered briefly across his features. 'Whatever else you may think of me, Kate, I'm not a bully. I'd like nothing better than to see Jim live out his days where he feels happiest. But I need to be sure he can do it in safety. I'd be failing as a doctor and as a friend if I did nothing and he had an accident or died from simple neglect. Surely you can see that?'

Kate turned her head to stare out of the window and was still pondering the problem when they drew up at the cottage ten minutes later.

Alice Tomkins, Jim's neighbour, opened the door as they reached it and led them into the small sitting room. A log fire crackled in the hearth but the room was still cold, made worse by a swirling draught which crept under a badly fitting door. A lamp cast a small patch of brightness into the early darkness of the afternoon. Jim Pearson sat in a chair, a blanket covering his knees.

'How is he?' Nick asked quietly.

'He was in quite a lot of pain this morning,' Alice Tomkins said, picking up a cup from the small table. 'I suggested he stay in bed. God knows, it would have been warmer.' She shivered, looking round the cheerless room and sighing heavily. 'I told him he should keep a good fire going, especially when the weather gets colder. But you know what he's like, Doctor—won't be told.'

Kate looked at the man sleeping in the chair and felt a tiny ripple of shock run through her. She remembered Jim as a tall and surprisingly strong man. Born and raised in the country, he had worked outdoors for most of his life, felling trees, coppicing and acting as the local water bailiff. Yet, suddenly, it seemed he had become a small, frail old man.

Nick put his briefcase on the floor. Sitting in the chair opposite, he gently reached out to hold one thin, blue-veined hand, his fingers registering the weak pulse.

As he did so, Jim's paper-thin lids flickered open.

'Hello, Doctor.' He blinked hard and smiled. 'I didn't hear you come in. I must have dozed off.'

'I don't blame you.' Nick grinned. 'It's nice here, in front of the fire.' He glanced at Kate, beckoning her forward. 'You remember Dr Jameson, don't you, Jim?'

Kate smiled. 'Hello, Jim. It's been quite a while since I last saw you.'

'Aye.' The old man frowned as he reached out to clasp her hand. 'I were right sorry to hear about your grandpa. How is he?'

She squeezed his hand gently. 'I think he's going to be fine.'

'That's good, that's good.' He looked at Nick. 'I didn't know you were coming out today, did I?' His blue eyes clouded with confusion. 'I must have forgotten.'

'I asked the doctor to call, Jim.' Alice raised her voice slightly. 'You had a bit of a fall, do you remember? You hurt your knee.'

'Aye. But that were nothing. No need to go bothering the doctor.'

'It's no bother, Jim,' Nick said gently. 'Is the knee still painful?'

'Aye.' Watery blue eyes gazed at him. 'Well, it always is, damn thing, so it makes no difference. It'll be fine.'

Nick smiled. 'Well, as I'm here anyway, suppose I take a quick look at it for you. See if we can do something about it. Is that all right?' He helped the man to

roll up his trouser leg, revealing a badly swollen, ar-
thritic knee, and Kate watched as he made his careful
examination, the strong hands moving with surprising
gentleness until he straightened up.

'Hmm, it's not looking too good, is it? It's badly
bruised and swollen.' Nick looked at the old man. 'You
have trouble getting round at the best of times, don't
you? And this certainly isn't going to help.'

Jim gave a rattly laugh. 'Just as well I weren't planning to go anywhere.'

'How do you manage getting out of bed in the morn-
ings?'

'I takes my time. There's nothing to rush for. I got
used to it anyway.'

'Yes, I can imagine.' Nick gave a slight smile. 'I'll
just listen to your chest.' He took the stethoscope Kate
held out and he made his examination, watching the
man's face as he did so. 'Yes, well, you are a bit rattly.
I think you've got a bit of an infection bubbling away
in there.'

Kate looked questioningly at Nick and as he nodded
she said gently, 'How do you manage for meals, Jim?'

'Oh, I do all right, don't you worry about that. Alice
here brings me a dinner.'

'That doesn't mean he eats it.'

Nick sat forward in his chair and looked directly at
the older man. 'You do know, don't you, Jim, that we
could arrange for you to go somewhere where you could
be looked after, where you wouldn't have to worry about
things like food or cleaning the house…?'

'I'm not going into one of those homes if that's what
you're trying to say.' The old man's eyes filled with
tears as Jim rested his head back and briefly closed his
eyes. 'I don't want folk fussing. I can manage.'

'All right, Jim.' Nick gently squeezed the man's hand. 'Don't you worry about it.' He shot a look in Kate's direction, nodding towards the door.

'You're not happy about him, are you?'

He lowered his voice as they moved away fractionally. 'I really don't think he's physically capable of looking after himself.' He frowned. 'Some days he can't get out of bed because of the pain in his hip. This accident isn't going to have helped.' He raked a hand through his hair. 'I can give him some painkillers but it isn't going to provide a long-term solution.'

'What are the chances of getting the hip operation brought forward?'

He gave a short laugh. 'What do you think? The trouble is, Jim's is just one name on a long list. I've written to the consultant again. I know they'll do what they can but I'm not too hopeful.'

'So what are you going to do? There's no way you're going to get him to agree to go into a nursing home.'

'The only thing I can do. Treat the pain as best I can and try to make him as comfortable as possible. I'll get the community nurse to call in whenever she's in the area.'

'You're assuming he'll actually agree to let her in.'

His mouth twisted. 'There is that, of course. I'll give him a shot of antibiotics now and prescribe a course of tablets for the chest infection.

'Would you like me to give him the injection?'

'It might be a good idea. At the moment I'm the villain of the piece. I'd rather not upset him any more. Kate?' Turning in the doorway she almost collided with his solid frame. He stared down at her and she saw him frown. 'Thanks—for coming with me. I'm grateful.' His thumb brushed against her cheek.

Confused as a strange new sense of awareness brought the faint colour to her cheeks, she lifted her face involuntarily to his. 'I don't feel I've really done anything to help.'

'You were here, that's what counts. Sometimes it's good to have a little moral support, don't you think?' His hand came briefly down over hers. She swallowed hard, feeling suddenly, ridiculously vulnerable.

Five minutes later they walked out to the car where Nick heaved himself into the driver's seat. His hands held the steering-wheel, his arms were taut, but he made no move to turn the key in the ignition.

Kate glanced at him and said quietly, 'You're not happy about him, are you?'

'Would you be?'

'No, probably not. But you did what you could.' She turned her head to look at him and frowned. 'Look, I owe you an apology. I shouldn't have suggested that you would act out of anything other than the best of motives where Jim was concerned.'

'Forget it.' He gave a crooked smile and brushed the back of his hand against his forehead. 'No one ever said the job would be easy. Sometimes you have to do things you don't like.'

Kate looked at him and felt a momentary flicker of alarm. He looked tired and pale. 'It's been a long day. Are you all right?'

'Fine.' He kneaded briefly at his eyes before reaching across to forage in the glove compartment. He produced a bar of chocolate, broke off a couple of squares and popped them into his mouth.

Kate stared at him and spluttered with laughter. 'I don't believe it. Dr Forrester, you're a secret chocoholic!'

'I skipped lunch,' he growled. 'Here, have some.' He thrust the bar at her.

She looked at it and grinned. 'Thanks, but I don't think—'

'Don't tell me you're on a diet.' His glanced flicked over her. 'There's nothing of you as it is. A puff of wind would blow you away.'

She felt the warm colour invade her cheeks. 'Oh, well, if it will ease your conscience…'

It was completely dark when, an hour later, they reached the hospital and made their way towards the cardiac unit where Sister Edwards greeted their arrival with a reassuring smile.

'He's sleeping peacefully at the moment.' She lowered her voice as they approached the bed where Alec lay with his eyes closed.

Kate swallowed hard. He still looked small and very frail.

Nick automatically reached for the clipboard at the end of the bed. He flipped the pages, studying the notes, and smiled. 'You're right, this is all looking very promising.'

'Yes, isn't it?' Sister smiled. 'We're very pleased with him. He's been sitting in the chair today, which is probably why he's tired now.'

'Has he had any more pain?' Kate said quietly.

'No, which is a good sign. We've even managed to persuade him to eat something.'

'I can hear you, you know. Alec opened one eye and grinned.

'Gramps! You old fraud.' Kate moved to the side of the bed and planted a kiss firmly on his cheek. 'I thought you were asleep.'

'I was pretending. It's the only way to get any peace

around here. There's always someone fussing. They keep giving me pills to swallow, taking my temperature.'

'They're doing their job. Humour them.'

'I hate fuss.'

'Some folk are just plain ungrateful.' Sister grinned. 'Look, I'll leave you to it.' She looked at her watch and headed for the door. 'I wouldn't stay too long. He's going to have a nice cup of cocoa and settle down for the night, aren't you, Dr Jameson?' She was gone, laughing, before he could frame a reply.

'You're incorrigible.' Kate sat beside the bed and held his hand. 'I suppose you realise you gave us quite a scare.'

He chuckled. 'I gave *myself* quite a scare. Anyway, this is a nice surprise.' He looked at Nick. 'I wasn't expecting any visitors. The day seems a bit long sometimes. I'm not used to all this inactivity.'

Kate felt her throat tighten. 'Oh, Gramps, I know how difficult it must be for you, but you're not to worry. Everything's fine at the practice.'

'My dear, that's one thing I've never had a moment's doubt about and, to be perfectly honest—' his blue eyes twinkled '—I'm almost ashamed to say I haven't missed it too much at all.'

'Well, that's good to hear.' Kate smiled. 'There's hope for you yet.'

'Just get well, Alec.' Nick also smiled. 'And behave yourself,' he advised, grinning as Sister Edwards approached. 'We wouldn't want to get on the wrong side of Sister, would we?'

'I should hope not indeed,' Shirley Edwards said with mock severity as she reached for the thermometer. 'We have ways of dealing with trouble-makers.' She smiled at Kate. 'Time's up, gentlemen, please, and now, Dr

Jameson, here's a nice cup of cocoa. Drink up then it's lights out.'

'You see what a bully she is?'

'I'll see you soon.' Laughing, Kate bent to kiss him. 'Sleep tight.'

Ten minutes later they were back at the surgery. Climbing out of the car, Kate reached for her bag. She felt drained and her head was aching.

'I think a strong cup of coffee is called for, don't you?' Nick led the way to the staffroom where he flipped the switch on the electric kettle and reached for the cups.

As he waited for the water to boil he turned to look at her as she shrugged off her jacket and delved in her bag for a couple of aspirin.

'Alec *is* in the best place, you know. He'll get the best of care and he is making progress.'

Kate smiled wryly as she went to sit at the table. 'I'm not sure he appreciates that right now.' She swallowed hard as her fear became almost tangible, something to be held off as long as she refused to give name to it.

'It's early days yet. Give it time.' He placed the cup of coffee in her hands, lowering himself into a chair and stretching out his long legs under the table.

'I know that.' She stared down at her cup. 'He just looked so...so different, so small. I couldn't bear the thought of losing him.'

'There's no reason to suppose you will, Kate. Don't torture yourself, imagining the worst.'

'It's not so easy, though, is it?'

Nick's hand reached out briefly to cover hers. 'He means a lot to you, doesn't he?'

'Yes.' She drew in a sharp breath. For the first time in a long time a sudden feeling of loneliness swept over her, threatening to overwhelm her in its intensity.

'Whenever I've needed him, Gramps has always been there for me. I was eight years old when my parents died in an accident. He took me in. He didn't have to but he chose to, and I grew up knowing that I couldn't have been loved more. And then…' Her throat tightened painfully.

Nick reached out to pour more coffee and for a moment she found herself staring at the dark strength of his arm. For one crazy moment she was tempted to reach out and touch it, as if in some way she could draw from it the strength she sensed was hidden there.

Instead, shakily, she ran a hand through her hair. Maybe she wasn't as strong as she wanted to believe.

Nick's fingers closed over her wrist, halting the movement. 'What happened, Kate?'

She tensed involuntarily. The past two years had taken the edge off the pain. It had become dull-edged but it was still something she found difficult to talk about.

'Paul and I…we were engaged to be married.'

'Were?'

She forced herself to look at him directly. 'Paul was killed, a month before the wedding.'

Some emotion flared briefly in the depths of his blue eyes. 'I'm so sorry. I didn't know.'

'There's no reason why you should.' Her chair grated noisily as she pushed it away getting to her feet. 'But Gramps was there for me again. I owe him a lot.'

Nick frowned and rose, too. 'What happened? Or would you rather not talk about it?'

She moistened her dry lips with her tongue. 'It was a motorcycle accident.' She pressed a hand to her mouth. 'Paul was something of a fanatic about them. I wasn't too happy about it but I could see it made sense. He was working as a registrar at the hospital. I'd only recently qualified and joined the practice here with Gramps. Paul insisted I use the car and he used his bike for getting to and from work.'

Her hand shook as she set her cup down on the table. 'The road was icy. His bike skidded, there was a lorry…' She lifted her head to look at him. 'Paul never regained consciousness. He died two days later—' She broke off.

'You don't have to go on. I shouldn't have asked.'

Sighing, she straightened up. 'It's all right. I don't mind talking about it.'

'Is that why you left Felldale?'

'I needed to get away. There were too many memories here. Too many reminders. Everywhere I turned. I needed some space, some time to think.'

'I can understand that,' he said softly. 'There are things we'd all like to run away from.'

Somehow she couldn't imagine Nick running away from anything.

'So, what will you do?' he said thoughtfully.

'I'm not sure.' She gave a slight laugh. 'I'd only planned as far as coming home to see Gramps. His illness has come as quite a shock.'

His gaze narrowed. 'I don't imagine you'll want to be tied down in a place like Felldale for long.'

Kate's chin lifted. 'You're making judgements but you don't know anything about me. Right now my only concern is Gramps. I just want to see him get well and I'll stay for as long as he needs me. I don't see that as a duty.'

'You might, given time,' he pointed out reasonably. 'In my experience people start out with the best of intentions, until other priorities get in the way.'

'But I'm not other people,' she retorted dismissively,

her tone faintly challenging. 'There's nothing more important to me than Gramps.'

'Except your career,' he tossed back, 'or your personal life.'

'Not even those.'

The twist of his mouth derided her. 'You sound very sure about that. Circumstances change. People change.'

Kate flicked him a glance. 'You're a cynic.'

'Put it down to experience.' He was standing with his hands in his pockets, staring out of the window. The stance seemed to emphasise the power in the shoulders beneath the jacket.

She wondered briefly who or what was responsible for the note of bitterness she had detected in his voice, then she brushed the thought away. What Nick Forrester did with his personal life was none of her concern.

With an effort she managed to force a smile. 'Look, I'm sorry. I didn't mean to sound so defensive, but all of this has come of a shock.'

'And I haven't exactly made things any easier, have I?' His mouth, a taut line of weariness, relaxed suddenly. 'Look, I'm sorry, too. Can I make a suggestion? Why don't we call a truce, start again? We have to work together and it will be easier, a lot less wearing, don't you think, if we can do so amicably?' Almost as an afterthought he held out his hand. 'What do you say? Shake on it?'

She stared at it, shock and surprise still warring within her.

As if Nick sensed her hesitancy, his gaze softened. 'I don't blame you for what you must be thinking.'

She started, feeling her colour rise at the possibility that he might have an inkling of what was going on in her head at that precise moment!

'Can't we at least give it a try?' He stood, watching as she tidied the cups away without really thinking about what she was doing.

His nearness was making her uneasy. Then, suddenly, his hand came down on hers, halting its movements, sending her gaze flying up to meet his.

She drew a deep breath and found her defences crumbling. 'All right. Why not?' Her breath caught in her throat as he stared at her and her pulse rate accelerated.

Someone tapped at the door and a spasm flickered across his features as she released her breath in a tiny hissing sound.

'Saved by the bell, I think,' he murmured wryly.

She did need rescuing, Kate thought, though not for the reason he imagined. Right now the air was charged with tension coming at her from all directions and she began to wonder precisely what she had got herself into!

# CHAPTER THREE

'AH, GLAD I caught you both. I needed to see you.' Huw Roberts's voice cut in. He smiled at Kate. 'Finished for the day, have you, *cariad*?'

'Just about,' Kate confirmed. Her breathing became more even as she found herself released. 'I've a couple of letters to write, but that's all.'

'I sometimes have this vision of life without paper-work.' Huw grinned. 'I reckon I could save a rain forest on my share alone.'

'You're probably right. Do you want coffee, Huw?'

'Well…' He glanced at his watch. 'If it's going. And maybe just one of those biscuits.' He helped himself as Kate poured the coffee and handed him the cup, careful to avoid Nick's glance in the process.

'You said you needed to see me, Huw,' Nick prompted. 'Was it urgent? Only I've a couple of calls to make.'

'No, not urgent exactly. I have this patient, see? Sixty-five years old, recently diagnosed diabetic—the maturity-onset, non-insulin-dependent variety. Chap's over-weight.'

'I take it he's been advised about diet and how to test his urine for sugar?'

'Oh, yes, and he seems sensible enough, but I thought it might be a good idea to refer him to your diabetic support group. I thought he might find it useful to talk to other folk in the same situation, especially with you being on both sides, so to speak. What do you think? I

know the clinic is pretty busy, but would you be able to
find a place for him?'

Kate's startled gaze flew to Nick, but his enigmatic
features told her nothing. He was a diabetic! For some
reason the idea shocked her. She felt she should have
guessed, even though, logically, she knew there was no
way she could have known. Diabetes was almost an in-
visible disease. In most cases it could be controlled so
that a patient might have the condition for years without
anyone else being aware of it. She wondered how much
more there was about this man that she didn't know.

'I'll make a place,' he was saying evenly. 'Talking
about problems is the best kind of therapy. From a
purely social point of view it's good for patients to realise they aren't alone.' He smiled. 'Just let me have his
details and I'll get Annie to send him an invitation.'

'Bless you. I appreciate it.' Huw looked at his watch
and put his cup down, stifling a yawn. 'I'd better go. I
promised Megan I'd take her out for a meal. Save her
having to cook.'

Kate smiled. 'How is Megan? I haven't seen her for
ages.'

'Oh, she gets a bit tired. Not surprising really. She
says the baby's kicking keeps her awake half the night.'

'She's pregnant! Oh, Huw, I'm delighted for you.'

Nick's eyes narrowed as he looked at the other man.
'Are you worried about her, Huw?'

'No, no, not really. Well, you know how it is. We've
waited a while for this baby. I'm thrilled to bits, of
course I am. We both are, but I'll be glad when it's over
and I know everything's all right.'

'Can you persuade her to rest more during the day?'

'Huh! It's a nice idea but you know Megan. Never
one for sitting still. Always got to be on the move. She

says I'm turning into an old grouch.' He grinned. 'She's probably right. Anyway, I'm off. I'll see you both to-morrow.' He kissed Kate on the cheek. 'It's good to have you back, *cariad*. Megan will be so pleased.'

'Give her my love.'

'Will do.' With a wave he was gone.

Kate looked at Nick and grinned. 'I'd no idea. I'm so pleased for them both. I know how much this baby must mean to them.'

He helped himself to a second cup of coffee. 'Of course, I'd forgotten you would know Megan.'

'I was in school with her sister, Laura. Megan was a few years ahead of us, of course, but we were all friends. We lost touch a bit while I was in medical school and, of course, Megan was doing her teacher training.' Her face clouded slightly. 'Does Huw really have any reason to be worried?'

'Probably not.' Nick looked at her from where he stood by the window. 'I gather they made a decision not to have children for a while. Megan was teaching.'

'Yes, that's right. She loved her work.'

He nodded. 'A few years ago it might have been quite unusual for a woman to have her first baby at the age of thirty-five. These days it's more the norm. Of course, the risk of having a Down's syndrome child are slightly higher, but Megan had the routine tests and they were all negative.'

'And otherwise she's perfectly healthy?'

'Seems to be. Unfortunately she did have a miscar-riage about twelve months ago.'

'Oh, no! Well, in that case I can understand why Huw is worried.'

'He thinks the world of Megan. It's a pretty rare thing these days to find a perfectly happy marriage.'

Again there was a note of cynicism in his voice, or had she imagined it? There was no way to find out as he looked at his watch and set his cup down.

'Time I wasn't here.' Nick moved towards the door, then paused to look at Kate. 'In case I haven't already said it, I'm glad you've agreed to stay as well. I know how difficult it must be for you.'

She gave a slight laugh as she gathered up her jacket and her briefcase and keys. 'Oh, well, I wasn't too keen on the other offer anyway.'

A faint smile twisted the corners of his mouth. 'Someone else's loss is our gain—for the next few months anyway.'

The genuine note of pleasure in his voice sent a tiny and thoroughly illogical frisson of happiness running through her, and she felt the faint tide of colour swim into her face as she sent him an answering smile.

'It's good to be back.' She had half turned away when her keys fell to the floor and the bundle of journals she had collected from the shelf began to slide from her fingers, crashing to the floor and scattering in all directions.

Annoyed with her own carelessness, she bent quickly to retrieve them just as he followed suit. Their bodies collided, momentarily knocking the breath out of her. She rocked backwards and instinctively he reached out, grasping her upper arms and drawing her towards him as he straightened up.

'Here, you'd better let me.' In one fluid movement he swept up the journals and placed them in her hands.

Kate felt the breath snag in her throat as, for several seconds, she was held within the warm circle of his arm. His skin smelled faintly of aftershave and she was totally unprepared for the primitive way in which, for those few seconds, she seemed to respond to that brief contact. She drew in a deep breath then pulled her hands out of his grasp. 'Thanks.'

'Think nothing of it.' His gaze narrowed. 'I'll see you in the morning.'

She nodded. Watching the door close behind him, she felt the first tiny feeling of pleasure fade. For a few minutes she had actually imagined he was welcoming her on a personal basis. On reflection she decided that Nick Forrester was simply pleased to have found a way of easing his own caseload. But, then, she reasoned, wasn't that precisely the reason why she was there?

It was evening and the air already struck with a deepening chill, heralding another frost, as she returned to the cottage.

Letting herself in through the front door she instantly began switching on the lights and put a tape of light classical music into the small radio-cassette before making her way to the kitchen.

A tiny, alien feeling of depression hit Kate as she shivered, realising that the boiler had gone out again. It probably needed servicing. Sighing, she made a mental note to do something about it as she showered and slipped a silk robe over her nightie. Thank heavens the emergency heater was working. I'll deal with the boiler tomorrow, she thought, along with a list of other things.

She felt exhausted as, ten minutes later, she padded over to light a free-standing gas heater in the sitting room and then into the kitchen to switch on the kettle before gazing optimistically into the fridge, trying to decide what to eat. Only to realise that she had forgotten to shop.

'Damn! Oh, well, one more for the list tomorrow. It

looks like it's going to be a busy day.' Sighing, she reached into the fridge for a wedge of less-than-fresh cheese and switched on the toaster, waiting for it to heat.

Carrying the tray into the sitting room a few minutes later, she sat on the ancient sofa with her knees tucked under her, a single lamp and the artificial flicker of the gas fire casting a subdued light into the room.

Sleepily, Kate rested her chin on her hand. It had been an odd, anxious and surprisingly eventful sort of a day, but she had coped, and in spite of her concern for Gramps she felt more on top of things than she had in many a month. Perhaps coming back to Felldale had served as a turning point, a final relinquishing of the unhappiness of the past and a gradual embracing of what the future had in store, even if it did, temporarily at least, include Nick Forrester.

She was taken unawares as a fleeting but nonetheless disturbing image of his attractive features flashed completely unbidden into her mind, and she wondered what it would be like to be married to such a man. The thought was crushed as swiftly as it rose. What was she doing, daydreaming about a man she hardly knew?

Her eyes must have closed because she started suddenly, jerking back to wakefulness and the realisation that someone was hammering at the door. Still half-asleep, she went to open it, gasping as a shaft of cold air hit her.

She felt her heart miss a beat. Nick stood there, faded jeans hugged his lean hips and thighs, emphasising his maleness. Beneath his black sweatshirt, his shoulders moved in taut definition.

He frowned. 'I was beginning to worry. I've been knocking for ages and couldn't get a reply.' His gaze narrowed. 'Are you all right?'

'What? Oh, yes. I'm sorry.' She ran a hand through her hair. 'I must have fallen asleep. I didn't hear you.'

'Obviously not.' His glance brushed over the robe she was wearing, and suddenly she was aware of how thin it was and how little she had on beneath it. 'I thought you might be able to use these.' He held up two carrier bags. 'It occurred to me that you probably hadn't had time to shop.'

Kate smiled. 'It didn't occur to me either, until I decided to raid the fridge. I was just about to start in on the chocolate biscuits. I appreciate the thought.'

He handed over the bags. 'It's only basics, I'm afraid. Milk, butter, eggs…'

'Basics sound fine. You must let me know how much—'

'Forget it,' came the quick rejoinder. 'I wouldn't want Alec to think I was neglecting you.'

She eyed him warily, then stepped back. 'Look, you'd better come in. It's freezing out there.' She clutched at the collar of her robe, drawing the edges together. Standing here in a partial state of undress wasn't doing anything for her peace of mind. 'Can I offer you a coffee? I'm afraid I don't have anything stronger…'

'I don't think so.' Nick's voice sounded a little strained, or maybe she had imagined it.

Kate stifled a yawn that made her eyes water. 'Sorry.'

A smile tugged at his mouth. 'It's been a long day.'

'And I need my beauty sleep.'

'I hadn't noticed anything wrong with the way you look.' There was a momentary pause, then he said briskly, 'I'd better go. I still have a mountain of paperwork to get through.'

'Me, too, but I think it might have to wait until tomorrow.' She stifled another yawn and watched him walk away before she closed the door. 'An early start. That's all I need.' She carried the bags into the kitchen, emptying the contents into the fridge, switched out the lights and made her way slowly up the stairs.

# CHAPTER FOUR

WINTER seemed to have set in with a vengeance the next morning.

Kate locked her car door and hurried breathlessly into Reception, her cheeks flushed with cold as she headed through the busy waiting room and into the office.

Carefully sidestepping a lively youngster, she put her briefcase on the floor and blew on her fingers before she pocketed her keys and reached across the desk.

'Sorry I'm late. I couldn't get the car to start. It doesn't like this weather.'

'I know the feeling.' Annie grinned. 'I can't get going till I've had at least two cups of coffee and even then there's no guarantee.' She handed Kate a stack of mail. 'It's looking pretty busy out there, I'm afraid.'

'Oh, great. Just what I need.'

'You'll be wanting these.' Annie handed over a batch of cards, smiling as an elderly man approached the desk. 'Morning, Mr Jeffreys. Take a seat. Dr Forrester will be with you in a few minutes.'

Juggling her briefcase and the cards, Kate tried to push a wisp of hair from her eyes. 'Nick's here already?'

'Don't worry about it. He reckons to get through more paperwork in the half hour before surgery than any other time.'

'I can believe it.' Kate's mouth twisted wryly. She glanced at the clock and groaned. 'I'd better go and make a start.' Not that she expected to be inundated with requests for her services, she thought. With Gramps out of the picture for the moment at least, Nick was sure to be flavour of the month.

A tiny feeling of depression homed in like a small black cloud as she shed her coat, checking her appearance in the mirror before pressing the buzzer to summon her first patient. Her cheeks were still flushed from the cold wind, adding emphasis to her green eyes. She flicked a comb through her hair and applied a touch of lipstick to her full soft mouth. Her gaze travelled briefly over the cherry-coloured polo-necked sweater and knee-length skirt. Moving to sit at the desk, she pressed the buzzer and waited.

All in all it was a busy morning, and it was a relief when she saw her last patient and was finally free to take a break.

Wandering into the staffroom, she found Huw already helping himself to coffee from the Thermos jug which had been left on a tray.

'I was just wondering whether I should send out a search party.' He grinned, helping himself to a chocolate biscuit. 'I thought I might just have to eat this lot by myself.'

Kate laughed. 'No chance. Mmm, I'm ready for this.'

Huw handed her a cup. 'So, how's it going, then? Gradually getting back into the swing of things?'

'Nothing much changes really, does it? The faces are a bit older. The children have grown. Ted Simpson still has his asthma and Mrs Lucas still has her dizzy spells.'

'Nothing new there, then?' Huw helped himself to another biscuit before handing her the plate. 'Sounds as if you're coping.'

'Oh, I'm fine really.' She sipped at the coffee, relishing its warmth. 'I could have done without the car playing up. It didn't exactly get the day off to a good start.'

'Problems?'

'Nothing that a major overhaul wouldn't cure.' She laughed. 'The poor old thing's past its sell-by date. I know I should trade it in but I just don't seem to get round to it. Anyway, enough about my problems—how's Megan? How long before the baby is due?'

'Not long. A couple of months. She says she feels fine.'

Kate shot him a glance. 'You don't sound too sure.'

'Well, I'll certainly be happier when she gives up work and starts taking things a bit easier.'

'I gather she's still teaching?'

'That's right. She loves it. I don't think she's exactly looking forward to leaving and sitting at home, waiting for this baby to arrive.'

Seeing the smile which didn't quite reach his brown eyes, Kate said gently, 'I heard about the miscarriage. Huw, I'm so sorry, but it doesn't mean things will go wrong with this pregnancy, especially not at this advanced stage. I'm sure Megan's been having regular check-ups and attending her antenatal classes.'

'Oh, sure.' Huw pushed a hand through his hair. 'Don't take any notice of me. I'll just be glad when it's all over, that's all. I keep asking myself whether we did the right thing, deciding to wait to have this baby.'

Kate smiled. 'Huw, Megan is thirty-five. A lot of women have careers these days. A lot of them choose to delay having a family. It's not unusual.'

'Yes, I know you're right.' He drained his coffee, staring at the empty cup. 'I know all the arguments.' He gave a slight laugh. 'That's the trouble with being a doctor, see? Always thinking about what might go wrong.'

'You need a holiday.'

'Ah. Don't we all? Still, maybe once we've got the

baby.' He smiled. 'Here, let me get you some more coffee while it's still hot.'

Kate was handing him her cup when the door opened and Nick walked in, a slightly harassed expression marring his attractive features.

'God, I hate paperwork. I seem to spend more time on it these days.' There was a taut edge to his voice. 'I should have been an accountant or an administrator instead of a doctor. If you're doing the honours I'll have mine black, no sugar.'

A small pulse began to hammer at the base of Kate's throat as she rose to her feet. 'I know what you mean,' she murmured, willing her hands to remain steady as she handed him the cup.

As he took it their fingers met, for some reason invoking so vivid a memory of the few seconds she had spent in his arms that she jerked away, spilling coffee into the saucer.

He was wearing dark trousers and a short-sleeved shirt. She found herself gazing at his hair, which curled slightly against his collar, before her gaze rose to meet the full impact of his startling blue gaze.

'Sleep well?' he asked.

'Like a log, thanks.' She took several deep breaths, hoping he would put the sudden surge of colour in her cheeks down to the hot coffee she had just swallowed.

'Actually, I'm glad I've caught you both.' Huw came unwittingly to her rescue. 'Megan wondered if you'd both like to come over at the weekend. She can't wait to see you again, Kate, catch up on some gossip and, as a matter of fact, it just happens to be our tenth wedding anniversary, so we thought we may as well mark the occasion.'

'Oh, Huw, yes, thank you, that would be lovely. If you're sure she feels up to it.'

'She's counting the days. If there's someone you'd like to bring along, feel free, of course.'

Without turning her head, Kate could feel the weight of Nick's eyes watching her, his own expression giving nothing away as she turned slowly. She found herself wondering, briefly, whom he would invite. Girlfriend? Wife? Her heart gave an extra thud, as she realised how little she actually knew about Nick. Without being aware of it, her fingers tightened round the cup.

'I haven't really had much opportunity to renew old contacts yet,' she said. 'Besides, from a purely selfish point of view, it will be nice to have a chance to see Megan again, just to be able indulge in a nice long chat.'

'Well, that's great. So I'll tell her it's on, then.' He grinned. 'And in view of the car situation, I'm sure Nick will be only too happy to give you a lift, won't you, Nick?'

Nick's gaze narrowed. 'Are you having problems with the car?'

'It's being a bit temperamental, that's all. I've arranged to take it into the local garage but they can't take a look at it until next week.'

'If you're really worried about it I'm sure they'll come to some arrangement about loaning you a replacement vehicle while they work on it.'

'Good idea.' Huw looked at them both. 'And in the meantime, there's no point bringing two cars when one will do, is there, and it's on your way anyway, isn't it, Nick?'

The set of Nick's mouth suggested that he wasn't at all happy about the way things were suddenly going.

'I'm not disputing that it's a good idea. It's just not quite that simple—'

'If you're worried about being on call, don't be. Chances are you won't have to leave early, but if the worst comes to the worst, I can always drive Kate home.'

'I'm not sure that's such a good idea. I imagine you'll be wanting to celebrate your anniversary with at least a couple of glasses of wine.' There was a distinct edge to Nick's voice now.

Kate felt the dull colour rising in her cheeks. 'Look, it's really not that important. I can quite easily make my own arrangement—'

'Don't misunderstand me.' Nick was frowning, a deep cleft between his dark brows. 'It's not that I wouldn't be happy to give you a lift.'

It's just that you'd rather not. Kate supplied the silent dialogue.

A spasm flickered across his features. 'Huw's right, it does make sense for me to pick you up. I just need to—'

'Please.' She bridled defensively. 'I understand perfectly. Don't give it another thought. Anyway, there's every possibility I may have had the car fixed by then.' If it hadn't fallen apart in the meantime! She pushed the thought away and, with an effort, forced a smile to her lips. 'Failing that, I'm quite resourceful. I can always get a taxi.' She saw a muscle tighten in his jaw.

'If you can just give me a couple of days to make some arrangements, then I'll let you know one way or the other.'

Confusion clouded her eyes as she acknowledged an inner sense of disappointment. Perhaps he resented the idea of being backed into a corner, or maybe he just disapproved of mixing business with pleasure.

She forced a smile to her lips as she gathered up her briefcase and made for the door. 'Yes, of course. But, as I said, it's no problem.' She flicked a glance in Huw's direction and saw a derisive smile tugging at the corners of his lips. She had the distinct impression that he was actually enjoying the situation, though why that should be the case she couldn't imagine. 'Thanks again for the invitation, Huw. Give my love to Megan. I shall look forward to seeing her soon.'

'Will do, *cariad*.'

It wasn't until Kate was seated in her car that she began to relax. She was annoyed with Huw for having provoked what had been an embarrassing situation.

On reflection, she thought, turning the key in the ignition and praying that the car would start, she wasn't at all sure that she liked the idea of mixing socially with Nick either. It could prove to be far too much of a distraction!

Making her way up the steps and into Reception next morning, Kate went to investigate the morning mail. Glancing perfunctorily through the batch of mostly brown envelopes, she sighed and consigned a proportion of it into the nearest wastepaper bin before glancing at her list of appointments.

'Any luck with the car?' Jill Stewart asked sympathetically.

'Oh, we had a slight difference of opinion again this morning. Still, hopefully it'll soon be sorted.'

Jill laughed as she handed Kate a folder. 'These are the letters you wanted typed. If you'd like to sign them I'll get them in the post tonight. Any news about Alec, by the way?'

'Yes, I rang the hospital first thing.' Kate glanced

through the letters, signed them and handed them back. 'They say he had a good night and seems much brighter.'

'Oh, well, that is good news.'

Probably the best thing that would happen all day, Kate thought as she reached across the desk to flip through the pages of the diary. 'Right, then, who's first on the list?'

'Mrs Lucas.'

'You'd better send her through then.'

It was a busy morning, with a steady stream of patients coming and going. The sudden onset of cooler weather had brought with it an inevitable rise in cases of bronchitis as well as an increase in the number of injuries caused by falls.

As her last patient left, Annie brought in another card. 'Sorry about this. It's Mrs Gibson. She doesn't have an appointment but she seems very anxious and I thought you'd want to see her. Would you like me to bring you a cup of coffee? I was just making some.'

Kate was tempted to accept the offer but she glanced at the list of calls she still had to make and shook her head. 'Better not. At this rate I'll be lucky to finish by teatime. What's the patient's name, did you say?'

'Mrs Gibson.'

'Right, you'd better send her in, then.'

Kate looked up, smiling, as the woman in question came hesitantly into the room. 'Hello, Mrs Gibson. Take a seat and tell me what I can do for you.'

Dawn Gibson, according to her notes, was thirty-five, petite and, if anything, slightly underweight. She moved slowly, almost nervously, avoiding Kate's gaze as she was directed to the chair.

'I'm sorry I didn't have an appointment, Doctor.'

'That's all right.' Kate smiled. 'If patients don't mind waiting a while when we're busy, we're always happy to see them. So, tell me, what's the problem?'

Dawn Gibson sat hunched in the chair. She stared at her hands, seeming uncertain where to begin. 'I had a bit of a fall, down the stairs.'

'I see.' Kate waited for some further response then, when none was forthcoming, she turned to her computer screen, quickly scanning the previous record of attendances at the surgery. 'And when did this happen?'

'A couple of days ago.' She moistened her dry lips with her tongue. 'I hurt my back, and my ribs.' One hand fluttered vaguely in the direction of her chest. 'It was my own fault,' she added with false brightness. 'I tripped over the damn cat. I just didn't see it.'

Kate swivelled her chair closer to look directly at the woman's lowered head. A yellowing bruise, barely covered with make-up in an attempt to camouflage it, was faintly visible as Dawn looked up.

'And is that how you got that? When you fell?'

'I expect it looks worse than it is.'

'I doubt it,' Kate said tightly. 'It must be painful. Do you have a headache?'

There was the merest nod of acknowledgement. 'It's not too bad. I've been taking aspirin, only they don't seem to help much.' Dawn looked at Kate. 'It's my back that's worse. I just need some stronger painkillers so that I can get back to work, see. Only I can't take any more time off…' She broke off to stare fixedly at her hands. 'I don't want to lose my job.'

'No, I can understand that.' Kate glanced at the woman's notes again. 'Where exactly do you work, Mrs Gibson?'

'At the pub.'

Kate nodded. 'And does it involve any heavy work? Any lifting?'

'Well, some, but not too much.' There was suddenly a note of panic in her voice. 'I'll be all right, Doctor, if you can just give me some tablets. I can't afford to lose my job. I need the money.'

'And you've taken time off before after you've had an accident?'

Dawn sniffed hard. 'Only when I broke my wrist. I couldn't work then.'

Kate studied her in silence for a moment, then drew a deep breath. 'What about your husband? Does he work locally, too?'

'Oh, Terry…he helps out his mates, fixing cars, that sort of thing. The odd building job, when he can get it. It's not easy. He had this bit of trouble, see? He got involved in a couple of dodgy deals.' Her voice broke off on something so closely akin to a sob that Kate had to resist the urge to reach out and hold the woman's trembling hand. She glanced up at Kate. 'It wasn't Terry's fault.'

'No, of course not.' Glancing at her notes again, Kate pushed her chair back and rose to her feet. 'Right, well, I'd like to take a look at your back. Chances are you did just bruise it when you fell, but I'd better check.'

'Is that really necessary?'

'Yes, I think so.' Kate smiled. 'I need to rule out the possibility of any broken ribs. Look, why don't you slip your blouse off?'

Panic widened the woman's eyes. 'I'm sure I'd know if I'd broken anything.'

Kate smiled. 'Not necessarily, and at least if we know what the damage is, you can adjust accordingly—per-

haps leave a few of the heavier chores for a while.
Maybe your husband could give you a hand.'

The woman's gaze slid away.

When Kate saw the livid bruises on the exposed flesh
she couldn't prevent a small gasp of horror. She studied
them in silence for a moment, then drew a deep breath.
'You say you fell?'

'That's right. Down the stairs.'

'Ah, yes, I remember. You tripped over the cat.'

Dawn gave a slight laugh and winced. 'Terry's always
saying I'm too clumsy by half.'

Kate said nothing. She was too busy trying to suppress
a growing feeling of alarm and anger. Her gaze rose
slowly. 'Dawn, these bruises weren't caused by a fall,
were they? Someone did this to you? Who was it?'

To her dismay, Dawn jerked away and began to re-
button her blouse. 'No. I don't know what you're talking
about. I told you, I fell.'

Kate swallowed hard. 'All right. But at least let me
check you over. I need to know what the damage is so
that I can prescribe the right medication.'

Dawn hesitated then nodded. 'OK, just so long as I
get the tablets.'

With an effort, Kate forced a smile to her lips. 'I
promise I'll try not to hurt you any more than is absolutely necessary. I just need to press here and…here.'
She heard the woman's soft intake of breath, saw her
eyes close briefly. 'I take it that's painful?'

'Phew! Just a lot.'

'Right.' Kate smiled and went to sit at her desk again.
'You can slip your blouse back on again now and come
and sit down.'

'So, what's the damage, then? Can you give me some
tablets?'

'I'll certainly write you a prescription for some pain-killers.' Kate frowned. 'Ideally I'd like to send you for an X-ray. There's obviously a very tender area just under your ribs. it's possible there might be a fracture.'

'No.' Dawn's hand came up sharply. 'I don't want to go to hospital. I can't stand them, they give me the creeps. Besides, I don't have time. There's my kid, Gary, and there's Terry. He won't be too happy if his dinner's not on the table when he gets home.' Her fingers drummed nervously on the desk. 'You said I could have the tablets.'

Kate saw the stubborn set of the woman's mouth and she stifled a sigh. 'Dawn, I'd like to help—'

'Then give me the prescription.' She was on her feet now. Her lips trembled. 'I hear what you're saying, but I don't need your help, Doctor. I'll be fine.'

Until the next time, Kate thought as she handed over the prescription. 'You know where I am…' The door closed before she could finish speaking.

Kate sat at her desk, willing her breathing back to a more even level. She didn't have a moment's doubt that Dawn Gibson had been lying. No fall could have caused the injuries she had seen, which could mean only one thing—she was lying, out of fear or to protect someone, and Kate couldn't do a thing about it.

She rose to her feet and drew a long breath, feeling frustration turn to anger. There was help out there for people like Dawn Gibson, but first they had to be per-suaded to accept it. Perhaps she should have tried harder, *found* a way. It was her job after all.

Kate replaced a book on the shelf, her movements oddly disjointed, then turned to snap the locks on her briefcase and gather up her keys and mobile phone.

Making her way to the office, she was hunting through

the filing cabinet and frowning when Annie came through from Reception. She dropped a bundle of case notes onto the desk and smiled.

'Can I help?'

'I'm looking for a list of local organisations and support groups.' Kate raked a hand through her hair. 'I'm sure it was always kept here.'

'Oh, yes, I know the one you mean. Yes, it was. Now, I'm sure someone asked for it recently.' Annie frowned, then snapped her fingers. 'Yes, that's right. Nick said he needed it. He's probably forgotten to return it, or it could be on the shelves in his room.'

'Do you know if he's finished surgery?'

'I should think so.' Annie glanced at the clock. 'I sent the last patient in some time ago, and I know he'd got a few visits to do. Is it urgent?'

'Mmm—it could be.' Kate pushed the drawer to a close. 'I'll see if he's still there. See you later.'

She walked along the corridor, coming to a halt outside Nick's door. Her heart thudded as her hand rose to knock. Did she really want the list so badly? Yes, she did, damn it. For her own peace of mind. For if—*when* Dawn Gibson had another 'accident'. Her hand hung, poised in mid-air. This was ridiculous. Sooner or later she had to face him.

She tapped lightly on the door and a tiny feeling of relief swept through her as no one answered. He was out, which meant that she could pop in, retrieve the list and return it later.

She pushed open the door, prepared to head for the shelves, and came to an abrupt halt, standing rooted to the spot.

Nick was standing at the desk. He had removed his jacket, his shirt was unbuttoned, revealing his bronzed, naked chest, and he was in the process of inserting a hypodermic syringe into an ampoule of insulin.

He turned, a look of surprise on his face, and said evenly, 'Did you want to see me?'

Her head rose and she felt the full weight of those blue eyes studying her. Warm colour flooded her face and she shook her head, backing towards the door. 'Yes—that is— Look, I'm so sorry.' Her voice sounded oddly husky. 'I thought you were out and I needed—'

'Kate, it's all right. You're not intruding.' His gaze travelled to rest on her face. 'I'm due an insulin shot, that's all. I wanted to have it before I go out on my calls.'

As he spoke, almost effortlessly it seemed, he injected the insulin subcutaneously into his abdomen, discarded the syringe and rebuttoned his shirt before turning to look at her.

'Sorry about that.'

'No, really. I shouldn't have barged in.' She moistened her dry lips with her tongue. 'I'd forgotten. It…it must be a bit of a nuisance.'

'I'm used to it. After a while it becomes just part of the day's routine.'

'How long ago were you diagnosed as having diabetes?'

'About three years.'

'It must have been quite a shock.'

He gave a slight smile. 'Not so much as you might think. My father had diabetes. I inherited it. I suppose, in a way, it gave me an advantage. I knew what to expect—the regime of regular blood or urine tests, the injections. Anyway, I don't imagine you're here to discuss my medical history. What can I do for you?'

Kate took the cue and dragged her attention back to

more relevant things. 'Yes, actually I was looking for the list of local support groups. Annie thought you might have it.'

'Yes, I do, somewhere.' He riffled through the papers on his desk. 'Ah, here we are. Sorry. I should have returned it.' He handed her the list and she glanced at it.

'It's no problem.' Now his smile, that was another matter altogether!

'By the way, you might like to know that I spoke to Sam Roach, the orthopaedics chappy, and he's agreed to bring Jim Pearson's hip operation forward.'

'Oh?' Her interest caught, she smiled hesitantly. 'And how many strings did you have to pull to arrange that, I wonder?'

His slow smile did things to her already overworked pulse rate. 'Let's just say he owed me a favour. But it wasn't just that. He remembered Jim anyway and he was I keen as I was, especially under the circumstances, to get it done as soon as possible.'

'Well, I'm glad. It's nice to know we're not entirely useless.'

Nick studied her, a frown briefly drawing his dark brows together. 'Kate, what's wrong?'

She moistened her lips, wishing there was some way she could avoid his shrewd gaze, but his hands caught at her arms as she tried to turn away. It was as if he had touched a nerve, sending tiny shock waves running through her. She drew a breath and shook her head.

'It's nothing. I can deal with it.'

'You're not a very good liar.' His eyes narrowed. 'What is it? Has something…someone upset you?'

Not nearly as much as his nearness was upsetting her nervous system right now, she thought.

'It's nothing.' She sighed. 'I just let something get to

me, that's all. I didn't handle a particular situation as well as I might have done and it made me feel, oh, I don't know...*angry* with myself.'

'I imagine we've all felt like that from time to time. Does this have something to do with the list you wanted?'

She gave a short laugh. 'I'm not quite sure what I had in mind, to tell you the truth.'

'Can you talk about it?'

She looked at Nick and ran a hand distractedly through her hair. 'One of my patients came to see me today, claiming to have tripped and fallen down the stairs, hurting her back in the process.'

'And you have reason to doubt what she says?'

Kate's gaze held his for a long moment, then she sighed. 'She agreed, reluctantly, to let me examine her. Let's just say that the injuries I saw aren't consistent with the story she came up with. For one thing they were too widespread. For another...'

'Go on,' Nick prompted.

She swallowed hard. 'They looked to me more like injuries that would have been inflicted by someone's hand or fist.'

'You're saying she'd been beaten up?' He frowned. 'I take it you voiced your suspicions?'

'Yes, of course.'

'And?'

'She denied it, of course.'

'Of course.' His mouth twisted.

'That doesn't make it any better,' she snapped peevishly.

'No, it doesn't.' Nick was watching her, a frown drawing his brows together. 'What about her previous medical history?'

'I checked. She saw Gramps about six months ago. On that occasion she claimed to have accidentally caught her hand in the car door. She had two broken fingers. And the time before that she slipped on a patch of ice.'

'It may have been true.'

She threw him a scathing look. 'You don't believe that.'

'What I believe doesn't matter. The question is, even if your suspicions are correct, what do you think you can do about it?'

'I don't know.' She stared at him. 'I just feel I should be able to do *something*.'

'Like what?'

She gave an exasperated sigh. 'Like... Like something. Anything.'

'Did she ask for your help?'

'No, but—'

'Then you don't get involved, Kate,' he said evenly. 'Unless she's prepared to admit there's a problem and chooses to do something about it, you have no business interfering.'

For a moment she stared at him in stunned silence. 'So, what are you saying? That I ignore it? Do nothing?'

'In a word, yes.'

'But that's... I can't do that. I can't just stand by—'

'Kate, you're not thinking rationally.' Suddenly his hands closed over her arms. 'You can't play judge and jury, Kate. You have to back off.'

But that was easier said than done. She strained backwards, her hands against his chest as she tried to push away from him. Frustratingly his grip merely tightened, sending a tingling awareness surging through her. It was crazy. She scarcely knew this man, yet he seemed to have the power to throw all her normally perfectly well-adjusted emotions into turmoil.

'I'm being perfectly rational,' she bit out. 'If I don't defend her, who else will?'

'But she hasn't asked you to defend her,' he challenged.

'Oh, typical! I might have known. You're a man and men are always rational, always tough. Or maybe that's just a cop out. It's so much easier, isn't it, Doctor?'

She knew it was a mistake even as she said it when his eyes narrowed to glittering blue slits.

'You're living dangerously, Kate,' he ground out. 'You're making a sweeping judgement based on what? You don't know anything about me, but one thing I can promise you. I can think of far better ways of getting what I want, without having to resort to violence. Perhaps it's time someone proved it to you.'

For an instant she thought of leaving, but knew it wasn't even an option as his grip tightened and he drew her towards him. She braced herself, her face flaming as he pulled her towards him, and she was fiercely, vibrantly aware of his strength, his powerful masculinity.

She tried to resist, her hands against his chest. He was devastatingly close, his touch firing her into tingling awareness. She gasped, panic briefly widening her eyes as he lowered his head and his mouth took possession of hers with an aggressive thoroughness, persuading her lips apart as his tongue invaded the soft vulnerability of her mouth.

She tried to twist away and for a second he released her, but only for a second as his gaze drifted down to dwell on the full curve of her soft mouth, and her heartbeat jolted to a jerky, staccato rhythm. Then, to her everlasting shame, a new and totally unexpected sensation forced its way into her consciousness, so devastating, so unlike anything she had ever experienced before, even with Paul, as her body betrayed her with its instant response.

'Maybe you don't know as much about me as you think,' Nick said huskily, a wealth of controlled feeling in the way he held her away from his body to look down at her. 'A little knowledge can be a dangerous thing, Kate. You should always be aware of your facts.'

Facts! Right now she was having trouble remembering what day it was.

He bent and kissed her again. His taste was warm and male and there was a hint of musky fragrance emanating from the pores of his skin. Her fingers clenched helplessly against the hard-boned contours of his shoulders as a wild, unbidden quiver of longing shuddered through her.

Moaning softly, she swayed towards him, surrendering to an overwhelming need. For an instant she felt him tense, then she was free, his breathing harsh as he drew away. She looked up, startled, a protest beginning to form, then became dizzyingly aware of the open door.

'Ah, Kate, Annie said I might find you here.' Huw's voice intruded into the tension.

Only then, as the brilliant colour swam into her face, was Kate aware of Nick shielding her from the other man's gaze, gaining her the precious seconds she needed to recover.

She dragged a hand through her hair, only too aware of how she must look. Her mouth felt bruised and swollen, her hair a wild tangle where Nick's fingers had run through it. All in all, she felt as if she had been ravaged!

'Not called at a bad moment, have I?'

'Not at all.' The sardonic gleam in Nick's eyes wasn't

lost on Kate. 'I was just clearing up a few points with Kate.' He turned to her. 'I think I've made my position clear, wouldn't you say?'

She choked. 'Perfectly, thank you. I'm sure there's no danger whatsoever of my forgetting…' But he was gone, without giving her a chance to explain.

She turned to Huw, with an effort keeping her voice even. 'Huw, you wanted to see me? What can I do for you?'

Huw's mouth quirked as he handed her a couple of paperbacks. 'I promised to let Alec have these. I know they're by his favourite author. And Megan asked me to tell you that she's looking forward to seeing you tomorrow. She can't wait to catch up on all the gossip.'

'I wouldn't miss it.'

'It's nothing formal. Just us and the neighbours and a few friends. How's the car behaving, by the way?'

She gave a slight laugh. 'Don't ask. Still, hopefully the garage will sort it out.' She moved towards the door. 'I wish you hadn't said anything about a lift. It may have put Nick in an awkward position. He and his…his wife may have had other plans.' The warm colour rose in her cheeks at the thought that she was so blatantly fishing.

Huw shot her an amused look. 'I shouldn't think that's very likely somehow.'

'Oh?' Kate felt her heart give an extra thud. 'I suppose with Nick being a doctor she's probably used to him being on call and having to work antisocial hours.'

Huw gave a hoot of laughter. 'I don't think that's likely to be a problem, not where Nick and Christina are concerned.'

A huge, suffocating cloud seemed suddenly to be hovering above Kate's head. Nick was married!

Even though she had half expected it, the sense of

shock hit her like a physical pain. With an effort she managed to force her lips into a smile.

'Well, it's not unusual these days for a couple to retain a certain degree of independence, especially if they both work.'

'Except that in Christina's case the independence was all a bit one-sided.'

'I don't understand.' The cloud shifted slightly. 'You mean…'

'Christina took off a couple of years ago. I don't know all the details. Nick doesn't talk about it and I don't ask, but I gather she decided the grass was greener elsewhere. As far as I know, the divorce came through about six months later.'

Kate could hear the deafening thud of her own heartbeat as a totally illogical sensation of relief swept over her. It lasted as long as it took to bring her breathing back under control. Nick might be free as far as the law was concerned, but he had been the injured party, the one left to pick up the pieces when the woman he must have loved had walked out. It wasn't very likely that he was going to want to get involved again, was it?

# CHAPTER FIVE

'GOOD morning, Sister.'

'Ah, Dr Jameson.' Smiling, Sister Edwards came towards Kate. 'You're bright and early today. I'm glad I
caught you.'

'It's my half-day. I thought I'd beat the rush.' Smiling,
Kate eased a stray wisp of hair behind her ear. 'Besides,
I've a bit of shopping to do. So, how is he today?'

'Quite bright. He actually sat in the day room for a
couple of hours yesterday.' Shirley Edwards popped a
pen into her pocket and frowned. 'I am just a little bit
concerned…' She indicated the office. 'Perhaps you'd
like to come in. Do sit down.'

Kate sat, though not happily. She tasted the sudden
dryness in her throat. 'In what way concerned, Sister?'

'That's the annoying thing.' Sister Edwards studied
the notes she picked up from the desk. 'It's difficult to
pinpoint anything specific.'

'Gramps is responding to the medication?'

'Oh, yes. We're certainly not at all worried in that
respect. He isn't eating a great deal, but that isn't really
a problem at this stage.' She flipped the page and looked
at Kate. 'To all intents and purposes he's making a
steady recovery from the heart attack.' She gave a wry
smile. 'Getting him to behave sensibly is another matter,
of course. Why, I wonder, do doctors always make the
worst patients?'

'I don't know.' Kate smiled. 'Perhaps they think they
know all the answers.'

'You could be right. It certainly doesn't make our lives any easier.' Sister became serious. 'I wish I could be more helpful. As I say, physically, Dr Jameson is improving. I spoke to him last night before I went off duty, and again this morning, and he seemed cheerful enough. I just wonder if something is worrying him. I could be wrong. It may be nothing, but obviously, if there is something, it won't help his recovery.'

'Perhaps I can get to the bottom of it.' Kate rose to her feet. 'I'll go and have a chat with him. You never know, it's possible he's worrying about the practice, in which case I can at least put his mind at rest on that score.'

Walking into the bright airy day room, Kate was able to study her grandfather before he became aware of her. He was sitting in a chair by the window. A newspaper lay open but ignored across his knees as he gazed out at the garden. She thought he was half dozing, but as she moved quietly towards him, he turned his head to look at her and smiled.

'Kate, my dear, this is a lovely surprise.'

'Hello, Gramps.' She bent to kiss him.

'You're nice and early. We've not long finished breakfast, such as it was.'

'Oh, dear, aren't they feeding you?'

He smiled. 'Actually, it's not bad. Things have certainly improved since my younger days.'

'I should hope so, too.' Smiling, Kate deposited some magazines and a bag of fruit on the table. 'I thought you might like these. Anyway, how are you feeling today?'

'I'm fine. Better every day.' He patted her hand and waved her to a chair. 'I get a bit bored. I was glad of those books Huw sent in.' He glanced at the garden. 'I shan't be sorry to get out of here. I never was one for being cooped up indoors.'

'No, I know that.' Kate leaned forward to pour him a drink from the jug, painfully conscious that he seemed thinner. 'I suppose there's not much point in my saying make the most of it while you can. Believe me, all you're missing out on right now is a chicken pox epidemic. If I've seen one spotty child I've seen a hundred.' She smiled. 'Give it time, Gramps. A few weeks and you'll be raring to go again.'

'I'm sure you're right, my dear. But if there's one thing I've had plenty of while I've been in here, it's time.' He smiled. 'I suppose the heart attack, and being in here, has given me a chance to do some serious thinking, to clarify a few things in my mind.' He turned his head to look at her. 'You don't mind, do you, that I asked Nick to take over as senior partner while I'm out of action? He's a good doctor, my dear, and he has the experience.'

She squeezed his fingers. 'Gramps, it's all right, you don't have to explain. Nick is the right person for the job. Of course I don't mind.' She looked at him. 'Is that what's been worrying you?'

He gave a slight laugh. 'Sister been talking, has she?'

'She's concerned about you, that's all.'

He frowned. 'I'm glad you decided to stay on for a while. Nick's going to need your support, especially when Megan has her baby. Huw is bound to need some time off.' He turned his head to look at her. 'I know how difficult it must have been for you, coming back to Felldale.'

'It wasn't really so difficult.' She looked at him and smiled. 'I'll never forget Paul, Gramps. He was very special but I've done my grieving. I've realised that life goes on, that *I* have to move on. I know that's what Paul would have wanted.'

'They say it gets easier.'

She glanced at him. 'You still miss Gran, don't you?'

'I don't think a day goes by when I don't think of her.' He gave a slight smile. 'I'm not convinced that it gets easier. I think you learn to live with it. But you never quite get over the shock of realising that all the plans you made are never going to happen. That's very hard.'

'Gramps…'

He patted her hand. 'It's all right, my dear. I'm fine, really. It's just that I've been sitting here, looking at my life. That's what happens when you've nothing else to fill your time. I don't know how many more years I might have but, however many it is, I've realised there are things I still want to do, things I've put off doing.'

'What sort of things?'

'I'd like to make time to go and visit your Uncle David and Aunt Judy.'

'In Canada?' She laughed.

'Well, why not?'

'Why not indeed?'

'It's been what…ten years since I last saw them?' Alec frowned. 'We seem to have lost touch over the years. It's so easy to do, Kate. The years just slip away. We're always too busy.'

'Are you going to write to them?'

He chuckled. 'I thought I might do better than that. I think I'll telephone—invite myself over to stay with my younger son for a while, when I'm feeling up to it.'

Kate laughed. 'Gramps, you're wicked.'

'I know.' His mouth twisted. 'But you know what?

I'm beginning to feel better already. In fact— Ah, Sister. I need to make a telephone call.'

Shirley Edwards glanced at Kate and raised an eyebrow. 'Feeling better, are we?'

Kate grinned. 'Oh, I think you could say well on the road to recovery.' She rose to her feet and kissed Gramps. 'I'll see you soon, then. And remember, no annoying Sister or you might never get out of here.'

Thirty minutes later she was heading for town where, having locked the car she hurried through the rain towards the main shopping area.

Surveying the meagre contents of her wardrobe the previous evening, the result had been every bit as depressing as she had expected, and she had come to the conclusion that there was nothing else for it—she was going to have to splash out on something new.

Buying one dress shouldn't take too long, she told herself. It should leave ample time for all the chores she had planned to do but somehow had never quite got round to.

What she hadn't counted on were the brightly lit, festively decked shops, and it dawned on her with a sense of shock that they were already gearing up for Christmas.

It was a newly opened boutique that caught her eye as she strolled among the lunchtime shoppers and, almost before she knew it, she found herself trying on a dress.

'It's a perfect fit,' the saleslady enthused. 'And that midnight blue really suits you.' The faint note of envy was completely lost on Kate.

She was right about the fit at least. Turning so that she could view the back, Kate studied the dress which emphasised her slender waist and hips. She must have lost weight. Twelve months ago she would have needed a larger size, and it did look good, she had to admit. Her thick, chestnut hair fell softly against her neck. Her cheeks, slightly flushed, did somehow emphasise the rare and startling green of her eyes. It was a dream of an outfit but the price, when she looked at the label, made her wince.

She pushed the thought away, realising that her thoughts had drifted. 'I do like it,' she murmured, still hesitating. 'I'm really tempted.' But do you *need* it? The voice of her conscience pricked the bubble of enjoyment. After all, it wasn't as if there was anyone she wanted to impress, was there?

She jerked compulsively back to reality, to begin fumbling with the zip. 'I'll take it.'

Ten minutes later she came out of the shop into the busy precinct and on impulse headed for the nearest café where she ate a large apple Danish, drank a cup of frothy coffee and chided herself all the way back to the car park.

It was early afternoon and the rain was gradually turning to snow as she dropped her parcels onto the rear seat before climbing into the driver's seat, shivering as she turned her key in the ignition.

Nothing happened. She stared at the dashboard in disbelief and tried again, and again, with the same result.

'*Come on.*' Her hands gripped the wheel in frustration. 'Don't do this to me, not now.' She turned the key again, flung the door open and climbed out to lift the bonnet, peering inside with a look of disgust. 'I don't believe this. Don't I treat you nicely?'

'Having trouble?' The quiet drawl came from behind her. She jerked upwards, cracking her head on the bonnet, and let out a yelp of mingled pain and frustration. 'Do you have to creep up on people like that?'

'I wasn't creeping,' Nick said evenly. 'You were so busy talking to yourself, you didn't hear.' He peered over her shoulder. 'Were you looking for something in particular?'

'How should I know?' She threw him a malevolent look as she nursed a tender spot on her scalp. 'It's what people do when a car won't start. They look under the bonnet.'

A glint of mischief lit his dark eyes. 'I think you'll find that only applies if there's a problem with the engine.'

'And I suppose,' she managed with an effort to keep her voice very cool 'you know what's wrong?'

A tantalising smell of aftershave drifted into her nostrils as he moved closer. He was dressed in a dark suit, the material stretched taut against the hard muscles of his thighs. He looked powerfully masculine. The blue eyes glinted.

'I could be wrong, of course.'

Kate gave a short laugh. 'Perish the thought. What are you doing here, anyway?'

He raised an eyebrow. 'Even I have to shop for life's essentials from time to time. Actually, I've been to see a patient and thought I may as well kill two birds with one stone.' He winced. 'Sorry, an unfortunate choice of words.'

He reached out a muscular forearm. She stiffened, feeling the breath catch in her throat. A glimmer of amusement flickered in his eyes before he bent forward to inspect something beneath the bonnet. 'When did you last check your battery?'

Colour flared defensively in her cheeks. She swallowed hard. 'I...I don't exactly remember.'

'Naughty, naughty, Dr Jameson.'

'Yes, all right,' she snapped peevishly. 'I'm freezing here. The point is, can you fix it?'

He gave a slight laugh. 'Is there any point my asking if you have any leads?'

'Leads?'

'Jump-leads.'

'Probably not,' she said flatly. 'Wh-where are you going?' She watched in consternation as he strode away, only to fling open the boot.

'Just as I thought. These...' he waved them in her direction '...are jump-leads. It's lucky I'm parked close by. If you hang on here I'll do some manoeuvring and we'll have it fixed in no time—hopefully. Just when did you say it was going into the garage by the way?'

'Next week.'

'I hope it lives so long.'

He was striding away before she could summon a response, and a couple of minutes later she turned the key again and this time the engine sprang into life.

Nick slammed down the bonnet and came to stand beside the car. 'That should get you home safely. If you have any problems call me on the mobile.'

'I'm sure I'll be fine.' Warm colour surged into her cheeks. 'Look, thanks,' she offered. 'It was stupid of me to let the battery go flat.'

'Forget it.' His gaze lingered on her slightly wind-swept hair.

She must look a mess, she thought, but, then, she hadn't counted on standing in a snowstorm. Her look dared him to say a word.

'You've done something to your hair. It looks different,' he said evenly.

'I had it trimmed.'

'I like it.'

'Perhaps I should visit the hairdresser more often,' she said edgily, and his dark eyebrows raised quizzically.

'Having a bad day?'

'Not particularly.' So why was she being so snappy? It seemed Nick Forrester had this effect on her. She tried to wind up the window but, frustratingly, he was leaning on it. 'I must have got out of bed on the wrong side.'

'I'm sure there's an answer for that.' He was looking at her, studying her intently. She glared at him, looking for some sign of amusement at her expense. His mouth was nerve-shatteringly sensual. Kate drew herself up sharply. 'I have to go. I've still things to do.'

'Wait.' His hand caught her arm, sending a mass of ill-timed signals firing through her veins. 'Tonight.'

'Tonight?'

'The party? Megan and Huw? I'll pick you up at about eight, if that's all right?'

Kate stared at him. 'But—I thought there was a problem.'

'I didn't say that. I said I'd have to sort a few things out, make some arrangements.'

She swallowed hard. 'You really didn't have to bother.'

'It's no bother, Kate. I'll see you at eight, then.'

He strode away without a backward glance, leaving her to wonder what he would have said if she had told him it was inconvenient.

It was late afternoon by the time Kate returned to the surgery to catch up on some paperwork, make several phone calls and dictate a letter of referral to a consultant. Carrying them through to Reception, she handed them to Annie. 'I'd like these to go in this evening's post, if you can manage it.'

'Will do. I'll get cracking on them now.'

'By the way…' Kate frowned. 'I don't suppose the report on Mr Jenkins's biopsy has come through yet, has it? Only I need it rather urgently.'

'I haven't seen it.' Annie riffled through a pile of papers on the desk. 'Tell you what, I'll phone the hospital now and see if they can fax it through for me, if that will help. I can always drop it off at your place on my way home.'

'You're an angel.'

Annie grinned. 'So I've been told. Don't worry. Leave it with me.'

It wasn't until she was driving back towards the cottage that Kate realised a niggling headache was beginning to make itself felt. Nervousness seemed to be pumping pure adrenalin into her system. This is ridiculous, she chided herself. You're behaving like a teenager about to go out on a first date! Except that there was nothing even remotely childlike about her responses to Nick Forrester.

Back at the cottage, the dress on a hanger, she indulged in a leisurely soak in her favourite perfumed bath oil in an effort to make herself relax. Half an hour later she stood in front of the mirror wearing the fragile lace undies which were also the result of her impulse buying. She was going to have to stop this, she told herself firmly.

Her make-up she applied slightly more heavily than she would have done during the day, with silver-grey shadow adding emphasis to her eyes, a touch of blusher for her cheeks and lipstick.

Small gold hoop earrings caught the light as she turned her head and stepped into the dress. For a second doubts came rushing in. Was it a little too startling? As she moved the fabric clung to her hips. The skirt was slashed at the front from knee-level down, so that as she walked it gave a glimpse of her dark-stockinged legs.

As she eased herself carefully into the bodice it clung to her breasts as if it had been moulded to her, a thin halter giving an illusion of safety, except that the illusion was too swiftly shattered. The zip had somehow stuck.

Craning her neck to look in the mirror, she gave a sigh of annoyance as she saw that it had somehow managed to tangle with the fabric.

She was struggling to ease it down again when she heard the arrival of a car and, seconds later, a ring at the doorbell.

'Damn! Let yourself in, Annie,' she called out. 'I'll be with you in a second. Take a seat.'

She heard the door open and close again. She glanced at her watch. It was still early. Time for a chat and a coffee.

Kate eased the bodice down again, sprayed a delicate mist of her favourite perfume behind her ears and, clutching the unfastened bodice to her, hurried downstairs.

'Annie, I'm sorry about that. I have a bit of a problem. Would you mind—?'

She broke off, feeling a rush of heat as Nick studied her with penetrating intensity. She felt the glittering sweep of his blue eyes flame over the creamy translucence of her bare shoulders and the curve of her breasts.

'You!' She swallowed convulsively. 'But...you're

early. I wasn't expecting you for another hour. I thought you were Annie.'

'Sorry to disappoint you. I'm afraid there's been a slight change of plan,' he said evenly. 'I had to do a last-minute visit. By the time I got away I realised I was going to be late, so it made more sense to pick you up first and then go back to my place to get changed. If that's all right with you?'

Kate wondered if she had imagined the slight note of satisfaction in his voice. 'As it happens, it looks as if I arrived just at the right moment. Can I help?'

Kate passed her tongue nervously over her lips, intensely aware of Nick and the subtle musky tang of his aftershave. 'I... It's the zip. It seems to be stuck.'

'Here, let me see.'

Heat flooded through Kate's body as he slowly drew up the zip on the dress, his fingers brushing against her skin in the process. 'There you go. All safe and sound.'

She moved away, feeling oddly breathless and anything but safe. She reached for her jacket then hesitated. 'Can I offer you a drink? Coffee? Or I think Gramps keeps some sherry—' She broke off, something in the flittering gaze that raked her from head to toe making her hesitate.

Panic hit her. She stared down at the dress, blushing as she remembered how little she was wearing beneath it. 'Is something wrong? With the dress, I mean?' Her fingers fumbled nervously, checking the zip. 'I could go and change. It won't take a minute.'

'Nothing's wrong. You look beautiful,' Nick said huskily. He took the jacket from her, draping it round her shoulders, his hands making brief contact with her flesh. She couldn't prevent a tiny indrawn breath. An involuntary shiver ran through her and, as if he was aware of it, something flared briefly in his eyes before he released her.

'I think we'd better forget the drink.'

She glanced anxiously at her watch and held it to her ear. 'It must be slow. I hadn't realised we were late.'

'We're not, *yet*,' he said tautly.

Kate swallowed hard, her breathing uneven as he ushered her towards the car, opening the passenger door and helping her in before going round to the driver's seat. It wasn't a small car, but he was still too close and still the most sexually exciting man she had ever met.

She felt relieved that he made no attempt at conversation as he drove. Her own thoughts were company enough. Too much was happening too fast. She was beginning to wish there was some way of getting out of going to the party, but there wasn't. Her one consolation was that there would be safety in numbers, though safety from what she wasn't quite sure.

Five minutes later the car turned in through large, wrought-iron gates onto a gravel driveway before coming to a halt. In the darkness she was only able to gain a vague idea of what the house must look like. She realised now that she must have driven past it almost on a daily basis without ever really having noticed it, partly hidden, as it was, by trees, but it was certainly large.

Nick switched off the ignition and turned to look at her. 'I'm really sorry about this. I just need to take a quick shower and get changed. I'll try not to keep you too long.'

'It's all right.' With an effort she managed to drag her mind away from a disturbingly powerful image of his taut, naked body, slicked with droplets of water. She stifled a groan and climbed out of the car.

She glanced at the house, noting for the first time that

there were lights blazing from behind closed curtains. He probably had one of those automatic timers that turned everything on, she thought. She'd meant to suggest the idea to Gramps but had never got round to it. It was certainly more welcoming than coming home to a dark house, especially in winter. Better still, coming home to a glowing fire, a nice meal, and knowing someone was waiting.

She shivered, suddenly, illogically reluctant to be alone with this man and, as if aware of her reaction, his arm came round her.

'You're freezing.' He glanced up at the clear sky. 'I think we're in for a frost. Come on, you'll soon warm up.'

The door was open and she stepped into a large, lighted hallway. 'I'll get Helen to make you some coffee. Or perhaps you'd like something stronger?'

'Helen?' Her feet seemed suddenly to be encased in lead.

Nick turned to look at her and his dark eyebrows rose mockingly. 'Did I forget to say? Helen lives next door. She's an absolute treasure who pops in and does various things for me.'

Kate's gaze flew up to meet his. 'Oh, really? How nice for you!' She couldn't resist the jibe and saw his mouth quirk.

'Why, Dr Jameson, what a nasty suspicious mind you have. As a matter of fact, I'd like you to meet her. Come on. I'll make the introductions before I rush off to get changed.'

He pushed open the kitchen door and smiled at the young woman who was just removing her apron.

'Helen, there's someone here I'd like you to meet. Helen—Kate, Dr Jameson. Kate—Helen Goddard, my girl Friday, Jill of all trades, guardian angel, without whom I'd probably cease to function.'

'Dr Jameson. Nick's mentioned you, of course. I'm so glad to meet you.'

Helen Goddard was tall, slim, around thirty, and she looked good in figure-hugging jeans. The word 'housekeeper' took on a whole new meaning as smiling brown eyes locked on a level with Kate's.

'Miss...Mrs Goddard.' Kate studiously avoided Nick's gaze as she offered her hand to the other woman. 'How nice to meet you, too.'

Helen reached for her jacket from a hook behind the door and Kate knew a moment's panic.

'You're not leaving?'

'If we can ever get organised.' Smiling, she lifted a small holdall onto the table. 'My husband will think I've gone walkabout. I'm afraid we're still trying to decide what to pack. You'd think it was for a week, not just one night.'

Kate flicked a glance at Nick, whose expression betrayed nothing except a smile.

At that moment a door burst open and a small, blonde-haired, dungaree-clad child, who couldn't have been more than about four years old, came rushing gleefully towards Nick, closely followed by a long-haired terrier who skidded across the wooden floor and began bounding excitedly at Nick's heels.

'Daddy, Daddy! I'm going to sleep at Helen's house and I drawed you a picture.' One chubby hand waved a large sheet of paper in front of her father's face.

Kate caught a glimpse of the colourful drawing of a stick-like figure with a thatch of what was clearly supposed to be unruly black hair, and found herself suppressing a grin.

She watched in rapt fascination as Nick gazed at the drawing in studied admiration as he swept his daughter up in his arms.

'Well, that's great, poppet.' He raised one eyebrow. 'I think maybe it's time I got a haircut, though, don't you?' He kissed her flushed, baby cheek. 'I can see you've been really busy. I think that's just about the best painting I've ever seen.'

He glanced at Kate. 'Perhaps I'd better make some introductions. Ellie, this is Dr Jameson. Kate, this is Ellie, my daughter.'

Blue, heavily lashed eyes, so like her father's, locked with hers and Kate felt as if someone had reached out and tugged at her heart. So this was Nick's child. Pale and blonde-haired, so unlike him in looks, and yet, without a shadow of doubt, his.

He looked up, his gaze locking intently with Kate's for a few seconds before his mouth tightened and he returned his attention to the child.

Kate swallowed convulsively, feeling hot tears pricking suddenly beneath her lashes. Very solemnly she shook hands with the child. 'Hello, Ellie.'

'Hello, Dr Jameson,' came the shy response.

Kate smiled. 'It's lovely to meet you, Ellie, and, please, I'm sure we're going to be good friends, so why don't you call me Kate? That is...' she glanced up '...if your daddy doesn't mind?'

His gaze narrowed briefly. 'I don't see why not. If you're happy with that.'

'And how old are you, Ellie?'

'I'm four.' The child displayed the spread fingers on one hand and frowned. 'When am I going to be five, daddy?'

'Soon, poppet.' He lowered his daughter to the

ground. 'So, what are we going to do with this beautiful picture, then?'

'It isn't finished yet.' Ellie spread the paper out on the kitchen table, revealing puddles of bright, wet colour. She studied the drawing earnestly, before adding another splash of brilliant yellow. 'That's Daddy's car.'

'Well, that's wonderful.' Smiling slightly, Kate bent down so that she was on a level with the small girl and gazed intently at the painting. 'And what's this one here?' She pointed to a pool of green.

'That's Scwuffy, of course.'

Kate's gaze flew up to meet Nick's. He made a slight sound in his throat and nodded in the direction of the dog who was busy exploring his empty food bowl and pushing it around the floor with his nose. 'That's Scw-Scruffy.'

'Ah.' Her lips twitched. 'Well, yes, now that you come to mention it, I can see the likeness. It definitely is Scruffy.'

The dog, hearing his name mentioned, clearly thought it was an invitation to play. He bounded round the kitchen, feet skidding, and produced a rag chew which he proceeded to offer to Kate.

'Get down, Scruffy,' Nick admonished firmly.

The dog obviously thought it was all part of the game and raced round, barking excitedly, in search of more toys.

'Scwuffy, get *down*!' One small chubby finger added emphasis to Ellie's command. The dog sank like a stone, rolled onto his back, paws in the air, tongue lolling as he gazed in adoring fascination at the child.

Nick gave a sigh of exasperation. 'I sometimes wonder just who's in charge in this house.'

Helen grinned. 'Oh, I don't think there's much doubt about that, do you?'

'And whose side are you on?' he shot back at her, with an easy familiarity that did something to Kate's heart. He glanced at his watch and looked at Helen. 'I'd better go and get showered and changed or we're going to be late. You're sure you don't mind having Ellie to stay over at your place for the night?'

'Mind? I'm looking forward to it.' She grinned. 'We're going to have a great time, aren't we, Ellie? Besides, my lot are counting on it. They think it's a great adventure.'

'You have children?' Kate asked.

Helen's smiling brown eyes met hers. 'Two. Alice is just five. She and Ellie are in the same class at school, and Daniel is seven.' Her mouth twitched. 'I think he's just beginning to decide that he's not into girls' games, but Ellie is an exception. He reckons she's the best thing since sliced bread. Anyway...' she gathered up her bag '...time we were going.'

Nick bent to kiss his daughter and she flung her arms round him.

Kate felt her heart melt at the scene. The two of them, so unlike in looks. She could only guess that Ellie must take after her mother, in which case Christina Forrester must be beautiful. She swallowed hard, shivering.

As if instantly aware of it, Nick straightened up. 'You're still cold. You need some coffee to warm you up. I'm sure Helen won't mind seeing to it while I go up and get showered. I'll be as quick as I can. Make yourself at home.'

Minutes later, Helen had gone, taking Ellie with her. Left to her own devices, Kate wandered into the sitting room, her eye caught by details. A large, open fireplace, gleaming brass. She ran a hand appreciatively over a small writing bureau. Carefully placed table lamps reflected in polished wood surfaces. There were pictures on the walls. It was a room which had clearly been furnished by someone with eye for quality and style. By the woman who had lived here?

The thought briefly marred her pleasure. She could hear Nick moving about upstairs, the shower running—the intimate sounds any married couple might share. Warning bells clanged in her brain.

'Pour yourself a drink,' Nick called. 'I think there's some brandy. I'll be down in a minute.'

Kate bent to ruffle Scruffy's fur as he settled at her feet. Her coffee cup was still half-full. She sipped at it, deciding to forego the brandy in favour of a clear head.

Setting her cup down on the coffee-table, she moved round the room, gazing up at the pictures, peering at the titles of books on the shelves, before returning to stand in front of the fire. She held out her hands, feeling its warmth. There was something almost hypnotic about watching the flames lick, red and gold, around the logs.

'Sorry I took so long.'

Kate looked up to see Nick standing in the doorway. His hair was still wet from the shower. He looked devastating, the dark suit tailored to complement his strong shoulders, trousers moulded to firm thighs.

Kate felt her breath snag in her throat. 'It's all right. I, er…made myself comfortable.' She looked round the room. 'You have a lovely house.'

His brows rose quizzically. 'You think so?'

'Don't you? Nick, it's beautiful.'

'It serves a purpose.'

She turned to look at him and gave a slight laugh. 'You're not serious?'

'Kate, it's a house. It's too big for Ellie and me. I've thought of selling, moving to something smaller, but Ellie is settled here. She's been through a lot. She's feeling secure now. I don't want to upset all of that.'

But what about *him*? she thought. What about *his* feelings? He still loves his wife, she thought. The house probably holds too many memories of the woman he had loved, *still* loved.

She searched every plane of his face. It was a wonderful journey which told her absolutely nothing, except that he had built a near impenetrable barrier around his emotions. If only her own were so well controlled!

She looked at him. 'Ellie is a beautiful child.'

'I think so.' He reached for the brandy, swirling the liquid in the glass.

'She isn't at all like you. I suppose she must take after her—' She broke off, appalled at what she had almost said.

'After her mother? Is that what you were going to say?' he prompted softly. 'Yes, you're right. Ellie is beautiful, just like her mother.'

'Nick, I'm so sorry. That was thoughtless of me, especially as—' She stopped again, realising that she was getting in deeper still. 'Look, I really am sorry. Huw told me about your divorce.' She swallowed hard. 'We weren't gossiping. I mean, I wasn't prying…'

'It's not a problem,' Nick advised her. 'You must know you can't keep a secret in a small community like Felldale. And you're right, Ellie does take after her mother.'

'You must have been devastated, about the divorce, I mean.'

He frowned. 'I'm not sure what I felt. In any case, there are two sides to every coin.'

Kate gave him a long, searching look and decided he must have become expert at keeping his emotions on a tight rein.

'There were probably faults on both sides. These things don't happen overnight. I was working hard at the hospital. I'd just landed a job as a consultant, which brought added pressures in time and responsibilities.'

'I'd say that goes with the territory. Surely your wife understood? I mean, she knew when she married you what the job entailed.'

'It's never that simple, is it?' Nick frowned. 'It was what I'd always wanted, always worked towards.'

'It's surely what training in medicine is all about. We don't go into it to stand still,' Kate snapped. Now why on earth was she getting so angry? 'We work to gain experience, in the hope that patients will benefit, otherwise what is it all for? Surely your wife must have known that?'

'Christina had her own career. There was no reason why she should share my enthusiasm.'

Kate looked at him, moistening her dry lips. 'I'm sorry. I assumed… I mean, I thought…'

'She was a very talented fashion designer. As a matter of fact, we met at a party to launch the opening of her first boutique. A friend had dragged me along. I must admit I wasn't very enthusiastic. I hung around for a while, nursing the inevitable glass of champagne, and I was just thinking about making my excuses and making a tactical withdrawal, when someone introduced me to Christina. I'd noticed her, of course.' He gave a short laugh. 'You couldn't *not* notice her. She was the most beautiful thing in the room. There was something about her. People seemed drawn to her. She enjoyed that—

being the centre of attention. And why not? Christina was a very sociable creature. She liked people.'

For a brief second a hint of cynicism darkened his eyes. 'She liked people who shared her particular interests, who could open particular doors. It just seemed that, after we were married, our lives simply began to go in very different directions.' His mouth tightened. 'She developed her own circle of friends and business acquaintances and a social life that went with it. That wasn't particularly a problem, until she began making trips to the States.' He gave a short laugh. 'I suppose it was almost inevitable that she would meet someone else, someone who could give her all the things I couldn't.'

Kate felt her anger stirring. 'But why do you blame yourself for what happened? Your job was important to you. She must have known that. What were you supposed to do? Give it all up?'

'Oh, I gave up believing it would have made any difference. Perhaps it was naïve of me to expect Christina to want the same things I did, to share the kind of life I wanted. The world was opening up for her. She had far more exciting things to do than being the wife of a doctor.'

An illogical flash of rebellion made Kate want to shake him. 'Tell me if I'm wrong, but I thought that's what marriage was all about. Sharing and being there for each other and…and being there for the bad times as well as the good.' She glared at him. 'I suppose now you'll tell me *I'm* being naïve or old-fashioned for thinking that way?'

To her surprise Nick gave a deep-throated chuckle. She felt her heart give an erratic thud as his eyes held hers, heard his soft intake of breath as his hand reached out to gently trace the curve of her mouth before he drew her towards him.

'There's nothing wrong with the way you think.' He bent his head, his breath fanning her cheek as his sensual mouth moved closer to her own. 'You're talking about happy ever after. I happen to be rather old-fashioned myself about certain things.'

'You...you do?'

'Absolutely,' he said huskily. She sensed a tautening of his muscles as his hands moved gently, drawing her closer, shifting along her arms to glide down the sensitive curve of her spine and the rounded swell of her hips.

Her treacherous body arched towards him, drawn into the warmth of his fire, a soft, trembling sigh on her parted lips. Her mumbled protest was absorbed, his hand moved the curving fullness of her breast and she moaned softly. Her head went back as she let herself be swept along on a tide of emotions.

Her senses felt drugged. Desire flared out of control. Her hands reached up, drawing him closer and with that vital, overwhelming awareness of her body's needs, another new sensation came homing in to her bemused senses. She was in serious danger of falling in love with Nick Forrester!

For what seemed an eternity she stayed in his arms, feeling the steady building of desire as it washed over her, threatening to drown her. Being a substitute might not be so bad. It would certainly have its compensations.

Kate drew herself up sharply, shocked by the thought. How could she even think that way? She wasn't about to offer herself up as some sort of consolation prize. There was no future in loving a man who could only think of her as second best.

The trouble was that fighting him might be a whole

lot easier than fighting her own feelings, especially as the warmth of his lips moved in again on her befuddled senses.

In desperation she tried to draw away. 'Nick, I don't think this is a good idea.'

'Oh, I don't know.'

'We're going to be late,' she said breathlessly.

'Kate...?' He groaned as she stirred restlessly in his arms.

It would be so easy to give in, to surrender and let it happen, she thought. But there was no future in it. No future at all.

Slowly he let her go. 'I wish we didn't have to go to this damned party,' he said through gritted teeth, leaving her with the feeling that she hadn't won the battle, merely postponed the war.

# CHAPTER SIX

'KATE! Oh, Kate, it so good to see you again. It's been ages.' Megan Roberts smiled as she greeted their arrival. Tall and slim, she looked stunningly attractive in softly draped trousers and a loose-fitting top. 'And Nick, too. I'm so glad you could both come.' She kissed his cheek then hugged Kate. 'I've been so looking forward to seeing you again. We've so much news to catch up on.'

Kate grinned. 'You look wonderful, positively glowing. Pregnancy obviously suits you.'

'Perhaps you can convince Huw of that.' Megan smiled wryly, resting a hand gently over her swollen abdomen. 'I think he's still in a state of shock.' Laughing she drew them both into the brightly lit hallway. 'I think he's more nervous about the whole thing than I am. Anyway, do come in and join the throng.'

She raised her voice about the music. 'I think you knew pretty well everyone who's here.' She led them into the sitting room.

Nick's mouth quirked. 'I thought Huw said this was just going to be a small party.'

'Yes, well, that was the idea. I'm afraid things seem to have got a bit out of hand.'

There were certainly more people than she had expected, Kate thought as they edged their way through the jostling crowd.

Almost immediately Nick was waylaid, and, involuntarily, she found herself searching for his dark head in the crowd.

'Kate.' A glass of wine was thrust into her hand. 'I've been keeping an eye open for you.' It was Huw, his face flushed, looking very different from his usual working appearance in casual, short-sleeved shirt and pale-coloured trousers. 'Come and meet a few people.' He kissed his wife. 'The two of you can catch up on the gossip later. Ah, Steven, meet Kate, Kate Jameson. Kate—Steven Hardy.'

Kate found herself shaking hands with a stoutly built, dark-haired man of about forty.

'Steven is our local bank manager.'

'Dr Jameson.'

She smiled. 'Please, call me Kate.'

'I gather you just moved back to Felldale?'

'Yes, that's right. My grandfather isn't too well, so I'm helping out at the practice for a while.'

'Ah, well, in that case perhaps we'll be seeing more of you. As a matter of fact I've been meaning to see someone about this backache of mine. Can't seem to shift it. Damn nuisance.' His hand moved to the small of his back.

Kate stifled a sigh and, with an effort, forced a smile to her lips. 'Have you tried taking paracetamol? Or there are a number of very good anti-inflammatory prod-ucts…'

'Tried most of them.' Steven Hardy drained his glass and looked hopefully around for another. 'Don't seem to touch it.'

'Kate, I should have said, you will help yourself to food, won't you?' It was Megan. She smiled. 'Steven, your glass is empty. There's a rather nice white wine. Do try it and let me know what you think. I know Huw would value your opinion.'

'Ah, will do. The white, you said?'

He moved away and Kate grinned as her friend slipped a hand through her arm.

'That was wicked of you.'

'I know, but I thought you looked as if you needed rescuing. Steven is a nice man, but he'll give you his medical history if you don't watch out. Seriously, though, do eat. I made all this food. I'm sure there's far too much and I'd hate to see it go to waste.'

'Not much chance of that I shouldn't think.' Kate smiled and gazed at the laden buffet table. 'You must have been so busy, Megan. It looks wonderful. I hadn't realised how hungry I was until now.'

She helped herself to a sausage roll. 'You haven't actually told me how you're feeling.'

'Oh, a bit tired—well, more than a bit.' Megan laughed. 'But, then, that's probably to be expected, carrying this extra load around.' She rested a hand on her stomach. 'I'm sure it's going to be a footballer. I wouldn't have believed how strongly it kicks.'

Kate grinned. 'Well, I imagine Huw will be pleased. I take it he's hoping for a boy?'

'I don't think he minds. Neither of us do, so long as it's healthy.' She smiled. 'I'll call in and see you for my next check-up, if that's all right?'

'Yes, of course it is. When exactly is the baby due?'

'Oh, about another six or seven weeks. To tell you the truth, I'll be glad when it's all over. And at least then Huw can stop worrying.'

Kate laughed. 'Being a bit over-protective, is he?'

'Just a lot. I suppose it's only natural. You wait till it's your turn.' She smiled at Kate. 'Do you want children?'

Kate swallowed hard. 'Yes, probably. Some day. The question hasn't exactly arisen yet.' She glanced up and caught sight of Nick's dark head in the crowd, found herself gazing in rapt fascination as he threw back his head, giving a deep-throated laugh. Her heart gave an odd little jolt.

'I hadn't realised the two of you were coming together.' Megan followed her gaze in open curiosity. 'I didn't know you knew each other that well.'

'Oh, no, we don't, not really. But my car's playing up and it seemed more sensible for Nick to give me a lift.'

'Well, all I can say is, it's nice to see him being sociable for a change. I wasn't even sure that Huw would be able to persuade him to come tonight.' Megan turned to study Nick and, almost by instinct it seemed, he looked in her direction. She raised her hand, smiling acknowledgement, then leaned closer to Kate. 'It seems such a waste.' She frowned.

'He is one gorgeous hunk of a man. He was totally besotted by Christina, of course. God knows why, but, then, they say love is blind. Huw tells me I shouldn't interfere, but I would love to see him get his life back. I've tried everything. Theatre tickets, dinner parties. You name it, I've thought of it. He's immovable.'

She shook her head and grinned. 'God knows, if I were single and not in an advanced state of pregnancy, I'd fancy that man myself. Don't tell Huw I said that. But just because some selfish—' Megan broke off, biting her lip. 'I'm sorry. I hate gossip, but…'

Kate toyed with the sandwich on her plate. 'If it helps, I do know about Nick and the divorce.'

'You do?' Megan's eyes widened.

'I didn't realise it was suppose to be a secret.'

'Well, no, I don't suppose it is. Only Nick doesn't usually talk about it.'

'I don't suppose he would have, only we happened to be at his place—'

'Really! Well, well. Tell me more.'

Kate smiled. 'Nothing like that. It's just that Nick had arranged to pick me up at my place, then he was called out. It just worked out better to pick me up earlier then go back to his place so that he could change, that's all.'

'Oh.' Megan looked crestfallen. 'I gather he's been thinking of selling the house.'

'I think he's concerned that a move might upset Ellie.'

'You've met her?'

'Yes. She's gorgeous, isn't she?' Kate swallowed hard on the sudden tightness in her throat. 'What I don't understand is how any woman could walk away from her own child.'

'I think that's what hit Nick hardest, too. I didn't know Christina very well, but I got the impression that she wasn't ever the maternal type. She had her job, then the new boyfriend came along. No competition. I think the only example of good taste she ever showed was in choosing Nick, and no one can blame her for that. Unfortunately she was thoroughly self-centred. Most people would have tried for a compromise over their careers, but not Christina.' Megan sighed. 'Personally I think selling the house would be the best thing he could do.'

Kate took a deep breath. She was confused by a welter of emotions. What she felt for Nick was far more than mere physical attraction, though that was certainly part of it. But what he felt in return was raw need. In spite of everything he couldn't let go—couldn't put Christina out of his mind.

Steven Hardy homed in on them, carrying two glasses.

'Megan, you were right about the white. Jolly nice drop of stuff. Kate, you must try it.'

Kate's hand tightened spasmodically on the glass, her smile as transparent as the liquid it held if anyone had looked closely enough to see. 'Steven, I'm not really—'

'Try a little cheese. Refresh the palate.'

Against her will, she found herself being drawn away. Megan threw her a sympathetic look before her attention was claimed by the ringing of the doorbell.

'So, tell me what you think. Fruity? Spicy? Maybe a little hint of honey?'

Kate sighed. 'I'm afraid I'm no expert when it comes to wines, Steven.'

'Ah.' He mopped his brow with his hanky. 'Of course, backache's more your line. I was wondering whether I might try a spot of osteopathy or manipulation? What do you think? Or maybe an X-ray might be helpful.' His hand came to rest on her arm, easing her towards him as guests moved towards the buffet table and, somehow, almost without being aware of it, Kate found herself being manoeuvred into a corner.

She decided she didn't like Steven. He was short, sweaty, arrogant, and his hands were beginning to annoy her. She started as the chubby fingers crept round her waist.

'I was thinking…perhaps I could make an appointment to see you one day—at the surgery, of course.'

'Of course,' she muttered through gritted teeth, removing his hand from the lower area of her spine.

He waved the bottle precariously in the direction of her glass. It was rescued by Nick, who seemed to appear suddenly at her side.

He stared down at her flushed cheeks, and her pulse rate accelerated dangerously. 'Kate, I need to talk to you.

There's a bit of an emergency. You will excuse us, won't you, Steven?'

Startled, she was aware of Nick's hand coming to drape itself loosely round her waist. It felt nice, protective. She could feel the tension in his muscles as he manoeuvred her away.

'What's wrong?' She looked up at him and felt her heart give an extra thud. 'It's not Gramps?'

'Alec is fine.'

A dancing couple jostled for space and Kate was suddenly aware of Nick's body pressed against hers. She darted a glance at him. Even in the half-light she could see the tension on his features.

She swallowed hard. 'Nick, what…?'

'Shall we dance?'

'Dance?' She stared incredulously at him. He wasn't giving her any choice. Her breathing was constricted as he took her in his arms, moving slowly rather than attempting to dance apart.

'What are you doing?' She looked up at him. 'I thought you said there was an emergency?'

'There is,' he growled softly. 'I thought you needed rescuing.'

She gave a short laugh. 'I think I could have handled the situation.'

'Believe me, I know Steven Hardy and you'd have been way out of your depth.'

But wasn't she already? The pressure of his hand on he back drew her close, moulding her body to his. His fingers began to trace slow circles over the thin fabric of her dress and she felt the heat of his touch run like a flame through her bloodstream.

'Wasn't that just a little devious of you?' she muttered breathlessly.

'Probably.'

She drew a sharp breath as his lips nuzzled teasingly at her ear. 'Isn't he going to be just a little bit suspicious?'

'More than likely.' He glanced at his watch. 'I think we've done out duty, don't you? I'll just make our excuses and we can bow out.'

'Oh!' She couldn't avoid the note of disappointment that crept perversely into her voice.

He grimaced ruefully. 'I'm on call after midnight. I'd hoped to be able to make other arrangements but it seems the on-call services are overloaded because of the bad weather.'

He swept her to a halt in front of Megan and Huw. 'It's been a great party, folks, but I'm afraid duty calls. We're going to have to love and leave you.'

'Oh, no! So soon?' Megan kissed Kate. 'We've hardly had a chance to talk.'

'You shouldn't be such a popular lady. Never mind, we'll catch up. Maybe we can have coffee, or lunch.'

'I'd love that.'

'I'll get your jacket.' Huw kissed Kate and was heading for the door.

'Don't worry,' Nick said. 'We'll collect it on the way out. You stay with your guests.'

It was all managed so smoothly that before she knew it Kate found herself seated in the car and the engine purring into life.

'Was it true?' she asked after a few moments. 'Are you really on call?'

'As it happens, yes.' He shot her a sideways glance that was laced with humour. 'Why? Did you imagine I was just looking for an excuse to leave?'

'The thought did occur to me.'

'It didn't occur to you that I might simply want to be alone with you?' he said quietly.

Kate darted him a glance and swallowed hard. 'I thought… I mean, I don't imagine that socialising has come high on your list of priorities, and you *were* more or less forced into it.'

The car came to a halt and Nick switched off the engine. It wasn't until she gazed out of the window at the unlit, unwelcoming darkness of the cottage that she realised she was home.

'Kate.' Nick's hand closed over hers as he half turned to look at her. 'I wasn't forced into anything. I went to this party because I wanted to. Yes, it *was* difficult after Christina left. But the truth is, we didn't socialise much even when she was here—not together anyway.'

A spasm flickered briefly over his face. 'She had her own circle of friends. I'm not apportioning blame. My job was never the nine-to-five variety. It took up a lot of time. It intruded into any kind of social life we might have had. If we went out there was never any guarantee that I wouldn't be called away on some emergency or other. In the end Christina decided it wasn't the kind of life she wanted. I can't blame her for that.'

'I'm sorry,' Kate said softly. 'At least you have Ellie.'

'Yes, I have Ellie, and I'll always be grateful for that. I can't imagine my life without her.'

Kate stared briefly, unseeingly out of the window, then turned her head to look at him. 'Didn't Christina fight for her? Surely she must have wanted her own child?'

He gave a harsh laugh. 'Oh, it occurred to her, though not for the reasons you might think. Christina saw Ellie as some kind of weapon to be used against me. She threatened to take Ellie to the States. I would have

fought her every step of the way. Christina knew that.'
He frowned. 'She might have won. I don't even care to
think about that.'

'So, what happened?'

'I don't think Ellie fitted into the boyfriend's plans.
There wasn't room in his schedule for a child, particu-
larly someone else's child. Christina made her choice.
She left Ellie and went for the lifestyle.'

He sounded quietly angry. The words were forced out
in a roughened undertone and, hearing it, Kate shivered
as she became aware, yet again, of the depths of emotion
he was capable of. It would be so easy to give in to this
man.

His mouth indented briefly as he watched the tide of
colour wash along her cheekbones. 'I'm sorry. I didn't
mean to say any of that.'

'Don't apologise. You've nothing to apologise for.'

He reached out a hand, his fingers brushing gently
against her cheek, setting her heart thudding from the
brief contact. Or maybe it was the effect of too much
wine? Either way, it was a dangerous combination.

'It's late,' she muttered huskily. 'I have to go.'

'Kate, wait.' He forestalled her attempt to open the
car door as he reached across. She tried to move away
but his hands gripped her shoulders. His dark, expen-
sively tailored jacket brushed softly against her skin. The
sensation was electric, sending dangerous signals to her
brain.

'Don't go.' Nick's warm breath fanned her cheek as
he began a teasing foray across her eyelids, her ear, the
hollow of her throat. His lips merely brushed against
hers, yet it was enough to make her feel as if her entire
body were on fire.

She could hear the discordant thudding of her own

pulse, feel the heat of his body permeating through his suit to her legs, making her all too aware of his arousal.

Kate moaned softly, a new kind of awareness bringing the colour to her cheeks. His grip firmed on her shoulders and she was shaken by the feeling of warm strength that seemed to pour into her as he lowered his head to kiss her again.

The sensation was exquisite. Kate's head went back. She could hear the muted drumming of her own heartbeat as his mouth claimed hers, cutting off the protest that rose fleetingly to her lips.

The kiss was a fiery, stormy possession, making her head swim, bringing with it the realisation that it was too late. She was already in love with this man!

For a second shock held her immobile. It wasn't him she wanted to run from, it was herself!

'Kate, I need you.' His hands raked through her hair, moved to her shoulders, following the curve of her breasts. 'Oh, Kate.'

The husky tones lapped at the edges of her resistance, while all the time his touch stirred her dormant senses to a growing, tingling awareness. She moved restlessly, searching for some kind of fulfilment that seemed only just out of reach, drowning in sensations unlike any she had ever experienced before.

'You must know how much I want you,' he rasped, his lips teasing against the full softness of her mouth as his hands finally released the thin strap of her dress to claim the curve of her breast.

The depth of her body's response shocked her. She didn't think she had ever known such instant, mind-shattering awareness as this, and it brought a shimmer of bewilderment to her eyes as she stared up at him in uncertain dismay.

It was all happening too fast. The fact that she was in his arms, that he was kissing her, didn't mean her feelings were reciprocated. He had been the injured party when his marriage had broken up, she had to remind herself. And in spite of everything, it was all too clear that he still retained strong feelings for the woman he had married, the mother of his child.

End it now, a warning voice rang deep inside her brain, before you get hurt. Her hands tensed against the solid wall of his chest beneath his jacket and she heard him groan softly.

'Kate…'

Her head was swimming. In desperation she drew away. 'No,' she said huskily. 'Nick, this is crazy. It won't work. It can't.'

He relaxed his grip to look at her with narrowed eyes. 'What are you saying?'

'Don't you see? I'm not Christina.'

His voice was rough-edged. 'You think I don't know that?'

Kate shook her head, desperately fumbling with the door handle. His hand brushed against her shoulder. Brief as it was, the contact was sufficient to trigger a whole lot of signals she was trying desperately to suppress and he wasn't making it any easier.

'I know what she meant to you,' she said bleakly. 'The only thing I do know is that I won't be used as some sort of substitute.'

She felt him tense. He stared at her, a nerve pulsing in his jaw, then, abruptly, he let her go.

'Nick, don't you see, I don't just want to be some sort of consolation prize?'

'You're right,' he rasped. 'I'd hate to do something we might both regret in the cold light of day.'

She stared at him, desolation dulling her eyes before she finally struggled upright, her fingers fumbling at the strap of her dress as she thrust open the door and stepped out of the car and, without looking back, let herself into the cottage.

It was almost a minute later before she heard him drive away. Only then did she release her breath on a deep sigh, wishing she had never met Nick Forrester, and knew that even that wasn't true.

# CHAPTER SEVEN

IT WAS almost a relief in the week that followed not to have time even to think about Nick. Far from abating, the chicken pox epidemic seemed, if anything, to be getting worse, emptying the schools and filling the surgery. The onset of winter saw an increase in the number of coughs, colds and sore throats, too, and Kate found herself facing real concern about her more vulnerable patients.

There was a lot to be said for afternoon surgery, she thought as, having parked her car, she sidestepped a large puddle and headed for Reception. A morning spent visiting Gramps and then catching up on chores might not have been quite the way she would have chosen to spend her time off, but it had certainly gone some way to lifting the vague cloud of depression which seemed to have been hanging over her for the past few days.

She walked into the office, smiling as she shrugged off her jacket. 'Hi, Annie.'

'Hi, you're nice and early. Probably just as well. It's already pretty full out there, I'm afraid.' Annie nodded in the direction of the waiting room. 'Huw's out on his calls. I doubt if he'll be back by the end of surgery and I don't think he's too happy about it.'

She handed Kate the mail and Kate flicked through it ruefully, recognising the inevitable promotions from various drug manufacturers detailing the very latest in new products and medical care.

'Oh, well, it looks as if I won't be short of reading material for a while.' She smiled resignedly.

'And Sue said could she see you for a quick chat? Preferably before surgery, if possible.' Annie handed her a note.

Frowning, Kate looked at her watch. 'Is she in yet?'

'I think I saw her heading for the treatment room about fifteen minutes ago.'

'Right, I'll catch up with her. Can you give me five minutes, then send in the first patient?' Kate picked up her briefcase.

'Will do.' Annie nodded briskly and reached for the phone as it rang, leaving Kate to head along the corridor.

The door to the treatment room was open and Sue Foster, looking very attractive in her dark blue dress, was busy preparing for the first of her patients.

'Hi. I gather you wanted to see me?'

Sue looked up with a smile as Kate tapped at the door. 'Oh, yes. It's about Mr Jackson. I've got his notes here somewhere.' She riffled through the cards on her desk. 'Ah, yes, here they are. He came in yesterday to have his blood pressure checked again.'

Kate frowned. 'Jackson. Fred Jackson. He started medication for hypertension about…a month ago?'

'That's the one.'

'Is there a problem?'

'Well, it's just that the results of his blood test have come back and his cholesterol levels are a bit high.'

'Hmm. How high?'

Sue handed her the buff-coloured card. 'About seven point four.'

'Ouch! Yes, that is high. Ideally it should be around four.' Kate scanned the notes and an attached computer printout. 'Have you had a word with him?'

'Yes, briefly. I told him I thought you'd probably want to discuss it with him, with a view to getting the levels down.'

'And how did he take it?'

'Well, I can't honestly say he was too happy about it, but I explained that it's usually quite simply a matter of a change of diet or, in some cases, means taking tablets, or a combination of both.'

Kate nodded. 'He's not overweight, is he, as far as I remember?'

'No. And I had a chat with him about his diet. He says he doesn't eat fatty foods if he can help it. No fry-ups or chips, that kind of thing. Occasionally he might have a bit of chocolate. No ice cream. So, basically, he wasn't too happy with the idea of being told he has high cholesterol.'

Kate laughed. 'I can't say I blame him. Still, it needs sorting. It's possible it's inherited. Does he know if either of his parents had high cholesterol levels?'

'He hasn't a clue. Mind you, he said his father died at the age of fifty-three, so it's possible he may have had a problem but no one was aware of it.'

Kate pressed the back of her fingers against her lips. 'I'd better see him. The sooner the better. Did you ask him to make an appointment?'

Sue nodded and flipped through the appointments diary. 'He's going on holiday tomorrow, so I booked him in for the day he gets back.'

'Great.' Kate glanced at the clock. 'I'd better make a start or we'll have a mutiny on our hands. 'No other queries, were there?'

'No, that's the lot. Oh, how's the car behaving, by the way?'

'Fine. Good as new. Well, maybe not quite as good

as new, but at least it should see me through the winter.'
She sighed. 'Then I suppose I'll have to give some serious thought to changing it. Look, I'd better go.'

'See you later, then.'

Five minutes later she rang the bell for her first patient. 'Margaret.' Kate took a deep breath, instinctively shifted everything even remotely movable out of
reach and smilingly invited the harassed-looking young
woman with her two children to sit. 'Come in and tell
me what I can do for you.'

'It's this headache, Doctor. I just can't seem to get rid
of it and it's making me feel really quite rotten. I feel
so tired all the time.'

I can believe it, Kate thought as she viewed the pale
face of the smartly dressed young woman in front of her
and noted the lethargic movements as she tried to re-
strain her boisterous three-year-old.

Kate had known the Lucases for some time. They
were a popular, hard-working couple, well known
among the local community. At the age of forty, Hal
Lucas had inherited his father's dairy farm and had
seemed to be making a go of things, so that it came as
something of a shock to Kate to see her patient looking
uncharacteristically under the weather.

'How long have you been feeling like this, Margaret?'

'Oh, a while. Kevin, don't do that.' She tugged inef-
fectually at her elder son. 'I'm sorry. He's not usually
naughty, just a bit lively.'

Kate smiled. 'Don't worry about it. I expect he's
bored, aren't you, young fellow? Here…' She reached
for the sweetie jar in which she kept a supply of jelly
babies. 'Try one of these. So, tell me about this headache, Margaret. When is it worse?'

'Well, it's difficult to say. It's there all the time really.'

'And when did you first notice it?'

The woman sighed. 'I suppose a couple of weeks or so ago.' She lifted the three-year-old who was squirming on to her knee. 'Look, I expect it will go. I usually take a couple of paracetamol…'

Kate let that pass while making a note. 'Are you getting enough sleep?'

Margaret Lucas gave a slight laugh.

'Not really. Oh, I drop off to sleep all right, the minute my head touches the pillow. You know how it is. These two keep me pretty busy.'

'Yes, I'm sure they do.'

'Trouble is I'm awake again in the early hours. It's ridiculous. I'm tired—worn out—but come three in the morning and I'm lying there awake, watching the hands of the clock go round.'

Kate pushed her chair back and looked at the pale, drawn features. 'Are you worrying about anything in particular?'

The woman looked away, picking up her son's gloves. 'I expect most folk worry about something or other, don't they?'

'I'm sure they do,' Kate said gently. She twirled the pen she was holding. 'How is Harry? I haven't seen him for ages.'

'He's fine.'

'Still making a go of the farm? He was setting up his own yogurt and cheese-making business last time I saw him, using the milk from your own dairy herd, wasn't he?'

Margaret's face crumpled. Fumbling for a hanky, she blew her nose hard.

'That's right. It seemed like a good idea. The bank agreed to back us. They were all for it, while things were going all right.'

Kate saw the brightness of tears in the woman's eyes. She said quietly, 'What happened, Margaret? Can you tell me about it?'

'There's not much to tell.' The children stopped fidgeting and were anxiously watching their mother. 'We really thought we could make a go of it. We'd been losing money on the beef sales. The bottom dropped out of the market, so it seemed sensible to concentrate on the dairy side, using the milk to make our own dairy products. It seemed like a really good idea.'

'I would have thought people would go for fresh, locally made products.'

The woman sniffed hard. 'So did we, and we were starting to build up quite a nice little business. But then some of the other farmers started doing the same thing. Well, you can't blame them, can you? In the end we were competing with friends just to stay alive. And then they went and built that big new supermarket just outside of town. That was it really. The business just tailed off, sales started falling.'

Kate bit her lip. 'Oh, Margaret, I'm so sorry. What will you do?'

'I don't know. One thing's for sure, we can't carry on as we are.' She dabbed the hanky at her eyes. 'Harry's talking about selling up. Someone might be able to turn it over to arable land. There's a lot of interest in organic crops. I don't know.'

She slid the younger child to his feet and stood up. 'Look, I'm sorry. I shouldn't have bothered you with this…'

'Nonsense. That's what I'm here for.' Kate sat forward. 'Look, Margaret, I know you're going through a really bad time. I know how difficult things must be for you, and for Harry. I'm loath to start you on a course of antidepressants. They would certainly make you feel better in the short term, but they won't solve the problems.'

'No, well, I wouldn't really want to take them anyway. Like you said, they won't make the problems go away.'

Kate smiled sympathetically. 'What I can do is to prescribe some mild sleeping tablets. If you can get a decent night's sleep, chances are you'll feel more able to cope with things during the day. And get Harry to come and see me as well, if he thinks I can help.'

Tapping out a prescription, she printed it out, signed it, handed it to the woman and rose to her feet. 'I hope things work out, Margaret. Come and see me again if you feel you need to talk.'

Having seen the family out, Kate rang the bell for her next patient. All in all it was a busy afternoon and another hour and a half before she finally tidied her desk and gathered up her jacket.

'All finished?' Annie smiled.

'At last.' Passing through Reception, Kate handed over the case notes and was just about to turn away when Nick came out of his consulting room. He was just seeing a patient out. His mouth was taut, his blue eyes hard.

On the point of turning away, she hesitated. She felt she should say something, *wanted* to say something, but what?

The distance that had opened up between them since that last meeting was like a huge void, and the pain she felt because of it was almost tangible. And it hurt, even if it was of her own making. Until she had sorted out her own thoughts, maybe things were best left as they were.

She gave him a remote smile and turned away.

'Kate, we need to talk.'

She stood at the desk, looking at him warily. Her emotions were so close to the surface that she wasn't sure she could be near him without rushing into his arms.

'I'm afraid I'm rather busy. Annie…' she looked at the girl behind the desk '…can you remind me tomorrow to get a letter off to the hospital about Mr Glover's X-rays?'

'Sure.' Annie's glance flickered between the two of them before she went to answer the phone. 'I'll make a note.'

'Thanks.' Kate looked at her watch. 'I'd better go. I'll never get through my visits at this rate.' She headed for the door. Nick followed.

'Kate, how's Alec?'

She sighed heavily and came to a halt, almost wishing she hadn't as it brought him tantalisingly closer. 'He's fine. Much better.'

'What's this I hear about a trip to Canada?'

In spite of herself she smiled. 'I'm not sure that it's imminent, but he seems to have decided that it's time he got in touch with Uncle David again.'

Nick frowned. 'David?'

'His younger son. My dad's brother. It's been ten years since he and Gramps last saw each other. I suspect Gramps's heart attack has made him reconsider his priorities.'

'Well, whatever, he's certainly looking brighter. I'm glad for you.'

'Yes.' She swallowed hard. 'How's Ellie?'

'A bit off colour. Nothing specific. She's got a bit of

a cold and it's making her a bit cross. Even Scruffy is keeping out of her way. Helen took her over to stay with her for a while.'

So that was it. He was concerned because Ellie had a cold. She said evenly, 'I wouldn't worry too much about it. Children are amazingly resilient. Well, you don't need me to tell you that. Give it a few days and I expect she'll be fine.'

He frowned again. 'I kept her home from school. That didn't please her either.'

'No, I don't suppose it did. She's a bright child. Still, I'm sure Helen will cope.' She glanced at her watch. 'Look, I'm sorry, but I really do have to go.'

His mouth tightened. 'Kate, we can't leave things like this. We have to talk. Can't we at least—?'

'Oh, Nick.' Annie came out of the office. 'Sorry to interrupt, but I've got Mr Ridgeway on the phone, about his wife.'

He swore softly under his breath. 'I'll be right there. 'Kate…' He flung her a look. 'Please. We can't just leave things as they are.'

But some things were better left alone, she thought. The fact that she loved him didn't mean she was prepared to step into someone else's shoes. What about her own feelings? Her own needs? There was no future in loving this man. No future at all.

'Kate?'

But she was already walking away, blinking back the tears as she closed the door firmly behind her.

It was dark by the time Kate had finally finished her calls and made her way back to the cottage. It had been a long, exhausting day and a niggling headache was beginning to make its presence felt.

A long soak in a warm bath helped to ease some of the tension in her muscles and, having changed into jeans and a chunky, cream-coloured sweater, she headed for the kitchen in search of food.

She eyed the remains of the previous day's casserole and decided to settle for cheese on toast. Half an hour later, a mug of coffee close to hand, she curled up in a chair in front of the fire and tried to relax.

In fact, it was easier said than done. Infuriatingly, images of Nick's taut face kept drifting into her mind. In fact, she decided restlessly, Nick Forrester was becoming altogether too much a part of her thinking lately, and she found the realisation deeply disturbing. How could the feeling have grown in so short a time?

She told herself that she respected his professionalism, but that was only a small part of it. Her feelings for Nick were unlike anything she had ever experienced before. Even with Paul she had never felt quite like this.

Maybe she should leave Felldale. Now that Gramps was well on the road to recovery there wasn't the same imperative to stay. Without any sense of false modesty, Kate knew that she was good at her job so that finding something new wouldn't be too difficult. Not having Nick as part of her life—now, that was an altogether different matter.

Lulled by her favourite classical music playing in the background, and the warmth of the fire, Kate closed her eyes. But the sudden feeling of depression wasn't so easily shut out. Neither did the fact that she knew it was illogical make it any easier.

She was a grown woman, not lacking intelligence, used to making decisions and sorting out other people's problems. Yet she was incapable of solving her own.

She blinked a sudden misting of tears from her eyes.

Maybe Gramps was right when he used to say half a loaf was better than none, but one thing was for sure— there was absolutely no future in loving Nick and receiving only half a love in return.

It must have been the hypnotic effect of the fire that made her drift into an exhausted sleep. Whatever the cause, her dreams were no less troublesome.

It was the insistent ringing of a bell which finally roused her, and she felt shaky and drugged as she reached out to silence the alarm. Except that it was the telephone.

She peered disbelievingly at the clock which now said nine-thirty. 'Go away,' she groaned into the cushion. 'I'm not on call. You've got the wrong number.'

Not on call. Her sleep-fogged brain latched onto the thought and she sat up shakily, aware of the sudden dryness in her mouth as she rose unsteadily to her feet and went to answer the phone. 'Yes, Dr Jameson speaking.'

'Kate, it's Nick.'

It was as if her dreams had somehow managed to conjure him up and her heart gave an unreasoned jolt.

'Kate, are you there?'

She raked a hand through her hair. 'Yes.' She glanced at her watch. 'Have you any idea what time it is?'

'I know. It's getting late, but can you come over? I need to see you.'

She drew a ragged breath. 'Nick, don't do this...'

'It's business, Kate, not personal.'

Of course, she thought. How could she have imagined otherwise?

His voice sounded rough-edged with tension. 'I'm worried about Ellie.'

Kate felt her stomach tighten in a painful spasm. 'Ellie? Why? What's wrong,' she asked hesitantly.

'She's running a high temperature. She won't eat. She's tearful.'

'Does she have a rash?'

'Yes—and, yes, it's chicken pox.'

'Have you tried giving her a dose of Calpol?' in spite of herself, Kate smiled. 'Come on, Nick, you're a doctor. You don't need me to tell you these are classic symptoms.'

'I know that.' His voice sounded strained. 'I'm not looking for sympathy, Kate. I'm calling because Ellie asked for you.'

'F-for me? But—'

'Don't ask, Kate,' he rasped. 'All I know is I've tried everything I can think of and I'm just about at my wit's end. I just wish...'

That his wife was still there? She batted the thought away.

'Will you come? I think what she really needs right now is a woman's gentle touch.'

'I'm on my way. I'll be about fifteen minutes.' But she was talking to herself. He had already replaced the receiver.

In fact, she made it in ten. The door opened as she reached it and Nick stood there. He was wearing jeans and a black sweatshirt. 'I'm sorry about this.'

'It's no problem.'

He stepped back, letting her in.

'Where is she?'

'In bed. It's this way.' He led the way up the stairs and paused outside the bedroom door. 'Look, I meant what I said. I really am sorry.'

'Nick. I care about Ellie, too.' She glanced up at him. 'Are *you* all right?'

He drew a deep breath and glanced at his watch. 'I'm overdue a shot of insulin.'

'Well, then, go get it sorted, Nick. It won't help you or Ellie if you're ill.'

He frowned. His glance brushed over her face and tousled hair, the jeans and old sweater she was wearing, and she was suddenly aware that she must look as if she had literally just tumbled out of bed.

'It just hadn't occurred to me that Ellie would think of you,' he said tersely. 'It seems I was wrong.'

Kate forced a slight laugh. 'I doubt if I figured much in the scheme of things. I think she just wants a little sympathy, that's all. And why not?'

He stared at her, his dark eyes narrowed. 'That you figured at all is something I wasn't prepared for.'

Kate ran a shaky hand through her hair. 'She's four years old, Nick, and she's feeling miserable.'

A smile tugged briefly at his mouth. 'So she thought of you,' he murmured thoughtfully, before letting his glance leave her face as he pushed open the door. 'Go and see her. Make like a doctor. When I try it she's not at all impressed. I'm just Daddy. I'll make some coffee.'

Ellie was lying in bed. Her eyes were closed, her small face was flushed and tear-stained. Scruffy was lying on the carpet beside the bed, his chin resting on his paws, eyebrows twitching. Kate put her briefcase down, slipped off her jacket, ruffled Scruffy's fur and sat beside Ellie.

'Hello, poppet,' she said softly as she took one small hand in her own. 'How are you?'

Fretfully, Ellie turned her head to look at her. 'Kate! I wanted you to come. I told Daddy you would. I 'spect he's cross!'

Looking at her, Kate felt her heart give an odd little

lurch. 'I'm sure he's not, sweetheart. He's just worried about you, that's all. He said you're not feeling very well. Can you tell me what's wrong—show me where it hurts?'

One small hand drifted shakily towards the blonde curls. 'Me and Scruffy have got a little hegate.'

Kate frowned. 'Hega… Oh, you've got a headache? Scruffy, too?'

'He's very poorly.'

Smiling, Kate glanced at the terrier who sat up, tail thumping the carpet as she brushed a hand through his soft coat. 'Well, Scruffy is looking much better, so perhaps we'd better just take a look at you and see if we can't make you better, too. What do you think?'

Ellie thought about it and nodded. 'My friend Sophie at school was poorly the uvver day. She was sick.'

'Oh, dear, was she?' Kate made a gentle examination of the child's ears and throat. 'And what was wrong with Sophie, do you know?'

'She got spots.'

'Ah!' Kate smiled. 'And have you got spots, I wonder?'

'I fink so.'

'Let's have a look, shall we?' In fact, it scarcely needed an examination to confirm Nick's diagnosis of an advanced case of chicken pox, but she made the usual investigations before straightening up. 'Well, young lady, Daddy's right. I think you—and Scruffy—have definitely got the chicken pox.'

Ellie's eyes widened. 'Will we have to have some medicine?'

'I can give you something to make your headache better.'

'And Scruffy's hegate?'

Kate grinned and reached for her briefcase. 'I'm sure I can find something for Scruffy.' She foraged through the contents of briefcase and found the bag of jelly babies she usually kept for just this sort of occasion. 'Do you think we might give Scruffy one of these? Would you like to choose?'

One small, chubby hand reached into the bag and selected two sweets. 'One for Scruffy and one for me. Scruffy likes the red ones.'

'Well, then, the red one it shall be. There you go. And now, young lady, what are we going to do about these spots of yours?' She reached for her prescription pad. 'Something for the headache, and something to stop the spots itching. What do you think?'

Ellie nodded, yawned and kneaded at her eyes.

Kate smiled, brushing a finger gently against the flushed cheeks.

'How about a nice drink of juice and then a little sleep?' Kate poured fresh orange juice from the jug on the bedside table into a glass, supporting Ellie as she drank greedily.

Ellie handed the glass back to Kate and looked at her. 'When Sophie was sick, she stayed at home wiv her mummy.'

'Did she, sweetheart?' Kate had to swallow hard on the sudden feeling of tightness in her throat.

'Yes. But I don't have a mummy because she went away. I 'spect she didn't like it when I got sick.'

'Oh, Ellie.' Kate felt the breath snag in her throat as Ellie suddenly sat up and flung her arms round her neck. She felt the warm soft cheeks against her own.

Her fingers smoothed the silky-soft curls and she felt the child's chest heave in a small sob. 'You could stay with me, Kate. You could look after me. Scruffy and me would like that.'

Oh, and so would I, Kate thought, feeling her eyes fill with sudden tears. 'I'm sure Mummy didn't leave because you were sick. It wasn't because of anything you did.' She floundered helplessly, realising she was getting onto dangerous ground. She had no idea how much Ellie knew about what had happened.

She kissed Ellie's cheek, heard a sudden sound and glanced up to see Nick standing in the doorway. His face was taut and suddenly she found herself battling to keep her own breathing even. How long had he been standing there? How much had he heard?

'Ellie, sweetheart…'

'You don't have to go.' The little fingers explored Kate's face. 'Daddy would like it if you stayed and so would I, and so would Scruffy.'

Kate flung an anguished look in Nick's direction and there was no mistaking the strain on his face.

'I'm afraid it isn't quite that simple.' Kate settled Ellie gently against the pillows and looked at the flushed little face. She sighed heavily. 'I have my own house, and my work, and Daddy has his work.' And his memories.

The truth was that nothing was simple any more. Her whole life had been thrown into confusion from the moment Nick had walked into it. She felt as if she were walking on quicksand, and the more she struggled, it seemed the deeper she was being sucked in.

She closed her eyes briefly and opened them again to find Nick watching her, his expression, as before, shuttered, telling her absolutely nothing. No help there, then.

Kate rose wearily to her feet and gathered up her briefcase. With an effort, she managed to smile. 'Time you got some sleep, poppet. I'm sure you'll feel much better in the morning.' If only she could say the same of herself.

Nick bent to kiss his daughter. 'Night-night, tiger. Sweet dreams.'

And what about my dreams? Kate thought as, minutes later, she climbed into her car and drove away. The trouble was, where Nick was concerned, out of sight was definitely not out of mind!

# CHAPTER EIGHT

ALTHOUGH she hadn't expected to, Kate fell into a deep sleep almost the instant her head touched the pillow. Exhaustion and tension had finally set in so that, for the first time in what seemed a long time, she slept soundly. So soundly, in fact, that it took several minutes for the loud shrilling of the phone to penetrate her sleep-fogged brain.

Groaning, she peered disbelievingly at the clock, which now said just after five o'clock. She felt shaky and drugged as she reached out a hand and fumbled for the receiver and said huskily, 'Dr Jameson.'

Minutes later she was struggling into her clothes and a jacket as the kettle boiled. She gulped scalding black coffee to wake herself up. Her bag was beside her car keys. Barely flicking a comb through her hair, she ran out to the car, gasping as a wave of cold air hit her.

As she drove she stifled a yawn, trying to concentrate on the road ahead, slowing where small pockets of freezing fog had gathered.

The Andrews were a couple in their early thirties, living on one of the new estates that had sprung up in the past two years on the outskirts of town.

The door of the neat, modern terraced house opened within seconds of Kate having rung the doorbell.

'Oh, Doctor, thank you for coming so quickly. I'm sorry to have to call you out. Do come in.'

'I gather it's your little boy?'

'Peter. Yes, that's right. He's through here.' Gail

Andrews led the way into the sitting room where her husband, Mike, was pacing the room with a flushed, coughing five-year-old in his arms.

He shot a look of relief in Kate's direction. 'Oh, thank God. Sorry, Doctor, but we've been at our wit's end, wondering what to do for the best.'

'Tell me what's the problem.' Kate put her briefcase down and unbuttoned her jacket. 'Why don't you sit down, Mr Andrews? Keep Peter on your knee—that way he'll be happier while I take a look at him.' She smiled at the child. 'Won't you, young man?'

'He seemed all right when he went to bed.' Gail Andrews hovered anxiously close to her son. 'He had a bit of a cold but then in the night he started this coughing and said his throat hurt. I gave him a dose of Calpol but it didn't really seem to help.'

Kate reached into her bag for her stethoscope. 'He's certainly not happy, is he? I'll just have a listen to his chest.'

'We tried to hang on until surgery opens, but we got really worried when the cough seemed to get worse, and it sounds so odd—more like a bark, if you know what I mean?'

Kate nodded. 'Yes, I do.' She reached for a thermometer and popped it into the child's armpit. 'Have you noticed any change in his breathing?'

Mike Andrews glanced at his wife. 'That's really when we decided we had to call you. It sounds as if he's struggling to get his breath. What with that and the coughing… He…he's going to be all right, isn't he, Doctor?'

'I'm sure he is.' Kate smiled what she hoped was a reassuring smile as she made a gentle examination for any swollen glands and managed, with difficulty, to peer into the youngster's mouth. He pushed her away as he drew another laboured breath and began coughing again, his cheeks flushed, his eyes watering from the effort.

'All right, young man.' Kate gently patted his back. 'I'll leave you in peace.' She retrieved the thermometer, frowning as she shook it down. 'Well, his temperature is up a bit and his throat is quite red. Hardly surprising really, with all that coughing.'

'So, what is it, Doctor? What's wrong with him?'

'I think Peter has croup.'

'Croup!' Mike and Gail looked at each other.

'I've heard of it but is…is it serious?'

'It's frightening rather than serious, particularly for the patient, because he's having trouble breathing. It's not very nice for you either, having to watch him struggle.'

'You can say that again.' Mike gave a slight laugh. 'So, what exactly is it?'

'It's caused by an infection, inflammation and swelling of the larynx—the vocal cords. That's what causes the laboured breathing and the cough.'

'Can you do anything about it?'

'Yes. I can prescribe an antibiotic which should get rid of the infection.' Kate reached for her prescription pad. 'In the meantime, there are a few things you can do to make Peter more comfortable.'

She wrote out the prescription and handed it to Gail. 'What I suggest is that you take Peter into the bathroom, turn on the hot water full force into the sink and shower. This will saturate the air with moisture. Keep Peter in the steam for about ten minutes and I'm sure you'll find it will help to ease the coughing. If it doesn't, I want you to call me again.'

She snapped the locks on her briefcase to a close.

'Apart from that, if you have a cool-mist humidifier you could use it in Peter's room. Keep him in a semi-seated position. Perhaps you could let him watch one of his favourite videos or something to distract him, so that he can relax. I suggest you try to get him to drink plenty as well. Water, juice, cola—but not milk—and don't give him any solids during an attack. Coughing may cause vomiting.'

Smiling, she rose to her feet. 'I'm sure you'll find he improves fairly quickly. If not, or if you're at all worried, please, call me.'

'We're really grateful, Doctor.' Gail's anxieties for her son were clearly alleviated, simply by knowing the cause of his distress.

'No problem.' Kate made her way out to the car.

She decided against going back to the cottage. There seemed little point in falling into bed, only to have to climb out again an hour later.

Instead, she headed for the surgery, telling herself that at least there were advantages in arriving early. If nothing else, she would be able to catch up with a backlog of paperwork which seemed to be accumulating at an alarming rate.

Driving along the narrow lanes as the first streaks of daylight were creeping into the sky, she had time to appreciate not only the beauty of the frost-whitened countryside but also the peace and tranquillity of a time of day before the roads began to fill with traffic as people set about the business of the day.

Or, indeed, the business of the surgery, which began with the first ringing of the telephone, and from then on continuing, seemingly without pause, until several hours later.

By the time Annie popped her head round the door

half an hour later, Kate was actually beginning to feel she was making some headway.

'You're an eager beaver. What's this, then? Couldn't you sleep or something?'

'Chance would be a fine thing.' Kate looked up, smiling. 'I was called out at five o'clock.' She stifled a jaw-cracking yawn that made her eyes water. 'The Andrewses' little boy had a nasty bout of croup.'

'Oh, poor little thing. Frightening for the family, I expect?'

'Well, at least they looked a bit happier by the time I left.' Kate leaned back in her chair and stretched her arms above her head. 'By the time I finally got away it was hardly worth going back to bed, so I thought I'd come in and catch up on some work.'

'Morning!' Sue smiled as she paused in the doorway. 'Someone's bright and early.' She glanced at Annie. 'Any customers for me yet? No? Right, I'm off home, then.'

'You should be so lucky!' Annie grinned and handed her a bundle of cards. 'All yours.'

'Lucky, lucky me. Right. Best not keep the hordes waiting. See you later, folks.'

Kate glanced at her watch and sighed. 'I suppose the waiting room is full, too?'

'Rapidly getting that way, I'm afraid.' Smilingly unrepentant, Annie indicated the morning mail. 'These are for you.'

Kate groaned. 'A bit more paperwork.'

'And you'll be needing these.' Annie handed her a pile of cards. 'Oh, and the blood test results you were waiting for—Mr Randall's—have come through. Ah, yes, here they are.'

'Oh, good. Anything else?'

'No. Oh, yes. Mrs Barker asked for a repeat prescription for the anti-inflammatory tablets you gave her a month ago.'

Kate frowned. 'Have you checked her notes?'

'Yes, and she's already had two lots. I thought you'd probably want to see her before you write another prescription.'

'Good. I know the tablets are probably doing the trick, but I don't want to keep her on them longer than is absolutely necessary. Can you ask her to make an appointment to come and see me?'

'Will do.'

Kate said casually, 'Is Nick in yet?'

'Mmm. I saw him come in through the side door about five minutes ago. He went straight through to his room.'

'Talking of which, I suppose I'd better make a move. This starting early is all very well, but I feel as if I've already done a day's work.'

'I know the feeling.' Annie laughed. 'Never mind, soon be coffee-time.'

It was a busy morning. Most of the patients seemed to be suffering from fairly minor coughs and colds and Kate found herself wondering why they didn't simply dose themselves with whichever remedy suited them best, rather than coming to the surgery. There was also a slipped disc, followed by a little light relief as Kate was able to confirm a pregnancy.

'Really? Are you sure?' Julie Watson was thirty-one years old and had been married for seven years. Kate glanced at her notes on the computer screen, noting that this was the woman's first pregnancy.

She laughed as she washed her hands and returned to sit at her desk. 'Absolutely no doubt about it. Your test was positive. Judging from your dates, I'd say you're about twelve weeks.'

'Wow! I can hardly believe it. And there was I putting it down to a queasy tummy or something I'd eaten.'

'It's a mistake anyone could have made, especially since you say your periods weren't particularly regular anyway.' Kate glanced at her notes. 'I gather you saw Dr Roberts about a year ago because you were worried that you'd been trying for a baby for a couple of years.'

'Yes, that's right.' Julie grinned, her cheeks flushed with excitement. 'We didn't plan to start a family straight away, you see. Phillip had just taken his final exams in accountancy, and I'd been promoted at the bank where I work. Well, we thought we'd give ourselves time to save a bit. You know, look for a small house. That sort of thing.'

'Perfectly understandable.'

'The thing is, when we decided the time was right to have a baby…well, it just didn't happen.' She frowned. 'Everyone said I was worrying for nothing. They all tell you it takes time, but after a year, when nothing had happened, I did start to get a bit panicky. I mean, choosing not to have a family for a while isn't the same as not being able to have children, is it?'

'No, I agree. It isn't.'

'So I had a chat with Dr Roberts, and he reassured me. He said these things do sometimes take time and just to try to be more relaxed about it.' She grinned. 'He was right.'

Kate grinned. 'I take it your husband will be pleased?'

'Pleased! He'll be thrilled. I'll phone him at work and make his day.'

Kate chuckled. 'Right, well, the important thing now

is to arrange for you to start regular antenatal care. Will you carry on working?'

'Oh, yes, until a few weeks before the baby's due anyway. Afterwards...' she smiled '...probably not. I've waited a long time for this baby and I intend to enjoy it.'

'I don't blame you. So, you'll need to come to the clinic once a month. Our nurse will weigh you. Bring a urine specimen with you. She'll need to check that. Obviously, as your pregnancy advances, you'll have to come to the clinic more regularly. I'll arrange for you to have a scan.'

'A scan? Why, there's nothing wrong, is there?'

Kate smiled. 'I'm sure everything is fine. The scan is a routine procedure. It gives us an idea of the baby's size and we can check that everything is developing as it should. We also need to know how many babies we're dealing with.'

Following Julie out into the corridor a few minutes later, Kate found herself smiling. It was too easy to forget that there were pleasures to be found in medicine, as well as the less happy events, and it came as something of a shock to realise that she actually envied Julie Watson.

Lost in thought, she turned, intent on grabbing a quick cup of coffee before doing anything else. Her tactic of careful avoidance where Nick was concerned seemed to be paying off and she was quietly congratulating herself when she collided with another figure.

She swayed, caught off balance, and instinctively Nick reached out, grasping her arm to steady her as he straightened up. He looked tired. Worse than tired, she was shocked to see he looked haggard and an indefinable sense of longing swept through her.

'Nick! I thought you'd gone out on your calls. How's Ellie?'

'Spotty but happier. Look, have you seen Huw?' he said grimly. 'I've just had a call from Megan.'

'Megan?'

He frowned. 'Yes. I need you to come with me, Kate. I'm worried about her. I've been trying to get hold of Huw for the past hour.'

'Isn't he on a one-day refresher course somewhere?'

'Oh, lor. Yes, I think you're right. Damn!'

'Nick, what's wrong?'

'I'm not sure. I got a frantic phone call from Megan. She thinks something's wrong with the baby.'

'Oh, no! But she's still got about six weeks to go.' Kate felt her stomach tighten. 'She's not in labour?'

'I wish to God it were that simple. She sounds as if she's panicking. I've told her I'm on my way. Annie's phoning round to try to see if she can get hold of Huw. In the meantime, it might help if you can come with me. She's going to need some moral support. I think we may have to move fast. Have you finished surgery?'

'Yes, I've just seen my last patient out.'

'Good. I'll fill you in on the details as we go.'

'I just need to get my bag and mobile phone. We can take my car.'

Mercifully it was only a short drive to Huw's house.

'Tell me what's happening,' Kate said as he drove.

He glanced at the dashboard clock. 'She's presenting with abdominal pains and bleeding.'

Kate drew a deep breath. 'Severe?'

He shook his head. 'No, but sustained. Apparently it started early this morning.'

'And she didn't do anything about it?'

'I think she thought it might just go away.'

'*Hoped* it might,' Kate said tightly.

The car drew up at the house and Nick cut the ignition. He didn't waste any time trying the front door, but headed straight for the rear of the house. 'Megan said the door's unlocked. I expect she'll be in the bedroom. She was using the extension when she called the surgery.'

Kate followed blindly. At one point she stumbled. Nick's hand shot out to steady her. She said breathlessly, 'I hope she's going to be all right. Having got this far…'

'The signs aren't good, Kate, not at this stage, in the third trimester.'

'Could it be something else—something unconnected to the pregnancy? Appendicitis?'

'Yes, it's possible. The only way we'll know for sure is to do a scan. But I have to say I'm not convinced. The symptoms don't add up. Wrong type of pain, wrong place.'

Kate drew a ragged breath. 'Are we talking about placenta praevia? It can happen, especially in the last thirteen weeks of pregnancy, that the placenta covers the cervix, then any change in the cervix, such a softening or dilating, can cause the placenta to separate from the uterus.'

'It's possible. But I'm more inclined to opt for placental abruption.'

He took the stairs two at a time. 'Megan!' He strode swiftly in the direction of the faint answering call.

'Nick? Oh, thank God. Through here.'

Kate gasped as she saw Megan lying pale-faced and tearful on the bed. One hand rested instinctively over her swollen abdomen. She gave a slight sob as they came towards her, her eyes wide with fear.

'I'm so sorry,' she said weakly. 'I don't know what's happening. The baby *is* going to be all right, isn't it?'

'It is if we have anything to do with it.' Nick was a man of speedy reflexes. In one calm, unhurried movement he sat on the bed beside her. 'I'm just going to check the baby's heartbeat to see what the little fellow's doing in there.' A few seconds later he straightened up. 'Right, well, that's not too bad.'

He half turned away, dropping the stethoscope into his bag, and said softly, 'Eighty.'

Kate drew a sharp breath. The baby's heartbeat should have been between a hundred and twenty and a hundred and forty.

She quickly took the other woman's hand in hers. 'Are you still bleeding?'

Megan nodded. 'Quite heavily. I…I'm not going to lose the baby, am I, Kate? Not now?'

Kate shook her head. 'He's fine, so far. There *is* a problem, but you did the right thing, calling us when you did. You and the baby are both going to be fine.' She shot a look at Nick. 'Aren't they?'

He looked at her and she felt the warm colour surge into her cheeks, knowing she was breaking one of the unwritten rules of medicine, which was never make promises you couldn't guarantee to keep. But if he was aware of it, there was certainly no sign as he said quietly, 'Yes, of course they are.'

'I don't understand what's happening to me.'

Kate sat and listened as Nick held Megan's hand and explained quietly and unemotionally.

'We think the placenta may be beginning to detach itself and break up. Ideally your baby isn't quite ready to be born for a few weeks yet, so we'd rather it didn't happen. But it seems this particular infant is in something of a hurry.'

Megan's mouth quivered on a tearful smile. 'So, what can you do?'

Nick held her hand. 'I've arranged for an ambulance to come and take you to the hospital. They should be here fairly soon. It may take a little longer because there's snow on some of the minor roads. In the meantime, I'd like to examine you. I promise I won't hurt you.'

Kate watched, fascinated, as the strong hands moved with surprising gentleness. Even so, Megan winced slightly, confirming their suspicion that the uterus was tender and contracted.

Nick straightened up, rearranging the sheet. 'That's fine.'

'What will they do when I get to the hospital?'

'My guess is that they'll opt to deliver the baby by Caesarean section.' He saw the hint of panic in her eyes. 'Now, you're not to worry about it. It's quite a straightforward operation and I know the baby will be premature, but he's a good size and the hospital have all the equipment necessary to look after you and the baby.'

Megan's face was pale, but she managed to smile. 'Yes, Huw took me for a visit to the maternity unit. I was impressed.' She gave a jerky laugh. 'I didn't expect to go in under quite these circumstances.' Her smile faded. 'I hope Huw gets here soon.'

'I'm sure he will,' Kate said reassuringly. 'Annie was contacting the conference centre. He'll probably be at the hospital before you.'

'In the meantime, the best thing you can do is try to relax,' Nick said. 'When you get to the hospital they'll send you off to sleep, and when you wake up it will all be over.'

He made it sound so simple, Kate thought a little later as finally they moved away from the bed, allowing the paramedics to take over. Because of her training she knew the risks involved, not only to the mother but in delivering a live, healthy baby.

She blinked warm tears from her eyes as, minutes later, she watched the ambulance drive away.

It was only later, after she found herself being ushered into the car, that Kate realised she had again been re-lieved of her car keys and was sitting in the passenger seat while Nick drove. It also occurred to her that she was happy to let him take charge.

Closing her eyes, she shivered as a build-up of tension set in and, without even being aware of it, she sighed.

'Penny for them.' Nick's voice, coming out of the semi-darkness, brought her back to reality.

'I was just thinking—this baby means so much to them. I'm not sure how I'd cope with something like that.'

'You'd find the courage from somewhere.' He half turned to glance in her direction. 'People do.'

'I suppose so.' But, then, Megan had Huw. It was ludicrous to find herself suddenly envying Megan, of all people. 'This is ridiculous,' she choked. 'I'm a doctor. I know we're not supposed to get emotionally involved.'

'Hey, come on. Even doctors have feelings, Kate. It *is* allowed.'

The car drew to a halt and she sat gazing out of the window, only then noticing that they were at Nick's house, not the cottage. But, of course, she realised, it made sense, since he had left his own car at the surgery.

She stirred reluctantly. 'I'd better go.'

'Come in for a coffee. I don't know about you but I need one and, frankly, I don't fancy my own company right now.'

Put like that, how could she refuse? Besides, she thought as he put the key in the lock and stood aside for her to walk into the house, Ellie would be home with the redoubtable Helen.

In fact, the house seemed strangely quiet. Kate turned to look at him. 'What happened?'

'Ellie's gone to stay with my parents for a few days. They leapt at the chance to have her—and Scruffy. I dare say they'll spoil her rotten, but what the heck! I must have forgotten to mention it.' He moved towards the drinks cabinet and poured two brandies. 'Besides, it gives me a chance to catch up on some paperwork.'

So why did she get the distinct impression that he missed his daughter? It might have been because he picked up a ragged-eared furry toy from the chair and stood gazing at it, a tiny frown etched between his dark brows. Or because his desk looked remarkably uncluttered for someone who pleaded pressure of work.

He proffered a glass.

'I thought you said coffee.'

'I decided we needed something stronger.'

She looked at him and thought, Right now I need to be in your arms. She sipped at the brandy, coughing as it burned its way down her throat.

'You miss Ellie, don't you?'

'Yes, I do. The house seems unnaturally quiet, not to mention tidy. But my parents dote on her and she needs the company. I don't think I realised quite how much until the other day. Until then I'd thought we were pretty much self-sufficient.'

'I'd say she's a very lucky little girl, having so many people who care about her.'

'So many people, but not the one person who really matters.'

'Oh, come on, Nick.' Kate set her own glass down. 'Give yourself some credit. You've done a great job so far. Ellie is a sweet child. She's well adjusted, happy. What more do you want?'

'It's early days. She's only four. There's going to come a time when I can't give her all the things she needs.'

'Yes, there is. But it's a long way off. In the meantime, don't put yourself down. Ellie's a child you can be proud of.'

'You're an expert, are you?'

Kate felt the warm colour surge into her cheeks. 'I'm being serious.'

'So am I.' His blue eyes looked frowningly into hers. 'There are things I won't be able to do for Ellie, questions I won't be able to answer. She'll need a woman to turn to.'

'You're making too much of it, Nick—looking for problems that don't exist except in your own mind,' she snapped, finding his nearness illogically unnerving. Why did everything about this man have to be so desirable?

She sighed without being aware that she did so. A nerve pulsed in his jaw, then he put his glass down and drew her slowly towards him.

'Kate, oh, Kate,' he said huskily. His blue eyes searched her face intently as he touched her cheek. 'Have you any idea how much I've wanted to do this?'

The effect of his touch was even more potent than the brandy could ever be. She drew a shuddering breath as his hand moved to caress her breast, shocked as the taut nipple flowered in instant response.

The effect was as devastating as it was confusing. Resistance was a word that seemed to have been wiped from her vocabulary. She must have been crazy to think she could remain indifferent.

Nick raised his head long enough to look at her, a question in his glittering eyes. She answered it breathlessly, tilting her head back to look at him, her hands against the solid wall of his chest.

'This is crazy,' he breathed harshly, before his mouth descended again.

She had to agree, it was utterly crazy.


It was later, much later, as she was thinking of going to bed, that the phone rang. Sighing, she went to answer it.

'Yes, Dr Jameson.'

'Kate?'

'Nick?'

'I know it's late but I thought you'd want to hear the news. Huw just called.'

She felt the breath snag in her throat. 'The baby?'

'It's a boy.'

She gave a short laugh of relief. 'Oh, thank God. How's Megan? How's the baby?'

'She's tired but fine. Glad it's all over, obviously. The baby is small. They'll keep him in an incubator for a few days, just to be on the safe side. But he's going to be fine.'

Kate swallowed hard. 'I'm so glad.'

'I knew you would be, that's why I didn't want to wait till tomorrow to let you have the news.' There was a brief pause. 'I'd better let you go then. Sleep tight, Kate, and sweet dreams.'

She wished. Oh, how she wished.

# CHAPTER NINE

'ALL right, Mr Daniels.' Kate followed her last patient of the morning into Reception. 'Give the tablets a try, but if things don't improve after a few days, do come back and see me again. And in the meantime, no more DIY.'

Tim Daniels gave a sheepish grin. 'The wife won't be pleased. I've been promising to put up those shelves for the last twelve months.'

'Well, in that case, I'm sure she won't mind waiting another few weeks.' Smiling wryly, Kate watched him limp out of the surgery. 'Some people never learn.'

She deposited a bundle of record cards and a cassette on the desk. 'There are a couple of letters of referral which need to go off. Not desperately urgent.'

Jill Stewart smiled. 'I'll probably be able to get them in the post tonight anyway.'

Oh, hi, I'm glad I caught you.' Annie came out of the staffroom. 'Mrs Bristow needs a repeat prescription for her indigestion mixture. I said she could collect it later today, if that's all right?'

'Yes, that's fine.' Kate recognised the name of one of the practice's more elderly patients who found it difficult to get into the surgery. 'I seem to remember... Yes, here it is. I signed it earlier.' She handed over the prescription. 'Is that it, then?'

'I think so.' Jill said then put up the SURGERY CLOSED sign and nodded in the direction of the nearest consulting room. 'Er, you might want to know, Alec came in about half an hour ago. I wasn't sure if you knew…'

'Gramps!' Kate stared at her. 'What—he's actually *here*?'

'Large as life.' Jill pulled a wry face. 'You obviously didn't know. I'm sorry. I hope I did the right thing…'

'You certainly did.' Frowning, Kate gathered up her briefcase. 'I didn't even know the hospital was planning to discharge him today. Where is he?'

'He disappeared into Huw's room. Said he had a few things to catch up on.'

Kate bit back an exasperated sigh. 'I'd better go and find out what he's up to.' She shook her head. 'What am I going to do with him?'

Jill grinned. 'I'm glad it's your problem, not mine. He's a stubborn man.'

'Don't I just know it. Oh, well, I'd better go and see what on earth is going on.'

She headed along the corridor, tapped at the door of the consulting room and popped her head round in response to his command to enter.

'Busy?' she asked pointedly.

Alec looked up and grinned sheepishly. 'Ah, I wondered how long it would take for the word to get around.'

'Gramps! What are you doing here? *How* did you get here? Shouldn't someone have told me you were coming home?'

Alec's eyes twinkled. 'I got here by taxi, after some very hard bargaining with that tyrant of a sister.'

Kate pressed a hand to her forehead. 'I don't believe this is happening.'

'Kate, my dear, there's nothing to get upset about. I couldn't stand it in that place a minute longer. I'm fine.'

'Are you?'

'Of course I am. I saw the consultant first, obviously.'

Someone tapped at the door and Nick popped his head round. 'Is it true? *Alec?*'

'Nick! Come in. I'm glad you're here. I was hoping to talk to you both.' Alec waved the stem of his empty pipe in the direction of the chairs. 'Why don't you both sit down?'

'Because I'm still waiting for an explanation,' Kate said roundly. 'How did you manage to get hold of your clothes?'

'Easy.' He was unabashed. 'You weren't with me when I went into hospital. Someone stowed my clothes in a bag and popped them into my locker.'

'You are incorrigible.'

'I can understand Kate's concern, Alec.' Nick said evenly.

She flicked him a look of gratitude before looking sternly at her grandfather. 'And just how did you manage to sweet-talk Sister into letting you go?'

'I simply agreed to spend a couple of weeks convalescing with my sister, your Great-Aunt Jessica, down in Cornwall.'

She fixed him with a direct look. 'You *agreed*?'

'Yes. Why not? It seemed like a good idea. I haven't seen Jess for a while. Besides, it will give me time to some more thinking and some planning.' He looked at them both. 'I really do need to talk to you. I know, I know…' He held up his hand, cutting short a protest. 'I've sprung this on you.'

'We're concerned for you, Alec, that's all.' Nick eased himself upright from where he had been half sitting, half standing against the desk.

'And I appreciate it. I want you both to know that I'm

grateful for what you've done, the way you've kept things going while I've been out of action.'

Alec sucked at the still unlit pipe, frowning as he ran a hand through his greying hair. 'The truth is, I've had a lot of time on my hands this past week or so, time to do some serious thinking, and I've come to a decision. I'm going to retire.'

Kate's throat tightened painfully. She flicked a glance in Nick's direction, saw him tense as he moved towards the desk.

'Alec, don't you think you should give yourself more time?'

The older man shook his head. 'As I said, time is something I've had plenty of lately.' He smiled slightly. 'I think the kind of experience I've had makes you reassess your priorities. Suddenly things that seemed important no longer are.'

'But…*retiring*? Gramps, you love your work.'

'True.' Alec smiled at them both. 'But I'm seventy-two, my dear. Oh, I dare say I could go on for a few years yet. The question is, do I *want* to? I wouldn't want to settle for anything less than a full commitment and this heart attack has made me realise that I would have to accept limitations.' He sat back and looked at them. 'I don't think it would be fair to ask the rest of you to carry me, professionally speaking.'

'Are you sure this is what you want Alec…'

'Times are changing, Nick. Medicine is changing, so are our patients' expectations. Besides…' he tapped the stem of his pipe against the palm of his other hand '…I do have a purely selfish motive for taking this decision, and I'd like you to hear me out.' He frowned. 'I've decided that there are things I still want—need—to do with my life. I don't know how much time I have. No, my dear.' He cut off Kate's protest. 'We have to be realistic. I just know that I have to make the most of whatever time I do have left. I want to see more of my family.'

'The trip to Canada?' Kate said quietly. 'To Uncle David and Aunt Judy?'

Alec Jameson smiled and nodded. 'I want to do it while I can. No good leaving it until it's too late then spending the rest of my time regretting it. So I'm going to do it now, well, fairly soon.'

Kate looked at Nick. She watched the varying emotions flickering over his face.

Nick dug his hands in his pockets. 'You've obviously thought things out, Alec, and I can't argue with your reasoning. If I were in the same position I think I'd probably make the same choice.'

'Thank you,' Alec said quietly. 'It makes it easier, knowing that I have your support and understanding.'

'How soon were you thinking of leaving?'

'Straight away.' Alec stared at his hands. 'The longer I leave it, the more difficult it will become.' He glanced up and smiled. 'I promised Sister I'd take a couple of weeks to convalesce. I've spoken to Jess—she's expecting me. And I've talked to David. He wants me to go out there as soon as possible.'

He looked at Kate. 'My dear, you being here has made things so much easier these past few weeks. I know that's selfish of me. But now I'm asking you if you'll consider staying on, joining the practice on a permanent basis again?'

'Stay on?' Kate gasped and closed her eyes briefly. He couldn't know what he was asking. She flung a look in Nick's direction. He had turned away and was staring studiously out of the window.

'I know it isn't fair to spring this on you like this,'

Alec was saying. 'But I hope you will at least consider it, Kate, my dear. You know the practice, the way we work. You know Huw and Nick.'

Oh, yes, that was certainly true. She wished she knew what was going on in his mind. If only she could see his face. She swallowed hard. 'Gramps, I don't know what to say.'

'I know you said your previous contract had ended and that you were considering another offer.' Alec was on his feet now. 'But we could use you here, Kate. Will you at least think about it?'

Nick turned to look at her, his eyes narrowed. Alec kissed her cheek. 'Don't make your decision now, my dear. I don't need to know for a week or so. After that, depending on what you decide, obviously the practice will have to start looking for someone to take your place.'

'I—I appreciate that, Gramps.'

He smiled. 'Right, well now, I think I'd better go home and start packing. Jess is expecting me and I imagine the two of you will have some talking to do.'

The door closed. Kate found herself the subject of Nick's intense scrutiny. His eyes were dark as he looked at her.

'I didn't realise you were still considering another offer.'

She swallowed hard on the sudden tightness in her throat. 'I've spent the past couple of years doing locum work. I decided it was time to start looking for something more permanent and an offer came up. I was keeping my options open, that's all. Then, of course, I came home and…'

Nick stood looking at her. 'I hadn't realised your decision would need such careful consideration.'

'I had no idea Gramps was thinking seriously about retirement. It's a shock—and coming back to Felldale to live…' She turned away, only to have him take hold of her arm, forcing her to look at him.

'Would it really be so difficult? Or maybe you were looking for something bigger, better than we have to offer?'

'That has nothing to do with it,' she ground out. How could she tell him the truth, that to stay, to have to see him, work with him every day, would be too much to bear? 'I… You don't understand.'

'You know it's what Alec wants,' he persisted. 'He's right, the patients know you, they like you.'

Damn it, did he have to make things more difficult? She didn't need these arguments. Kate closed her eyes in a brief and utterly futile attempt to shut him out of her thoughts. She might have known it wouldn't work. How could it, when he only had to be within touching distance for her heart to start racing?

She jerked her eyes open, deciding that, in this instance, attack was the best form of defence. 'Be careful, Nick, I might just get the idea that you actually want me to stay.'

He frowned, his dark brows drawing together. 'It's your decision,' he said abruptly. 'I can't help.'

Can't, or won't? she felt like shouting. Tell me what you want me to do, Nick. Tell me to stay.

She stepped back, knowing that if she was to think rationally she would do it a whole lot more clearly away from him.

She drew a ragged breath. 'I need some time to think.' She backed away, moving towards the door. 'Don't worry, I'll let you have my answer as quickly as possi-

ble, so that you'll still have time to find a replacement.'
She turned away.

'Kate!'

She sighed, but hesitated at the door. 'Nick, please,
don't—'

'We can't leave things like this.'

Her hand tightened spasmodically on the doorhandle
and she thought, Don't do this to me, Nick. What I need
right now is a clear head.

'Have dinner with me, that's all I'm asking.'

Kate sighed. He made it sound so simple. On the other
hand, what had she to lose? Maybe it was simple after
all. She had a decision to make. Go, or stay. Easy.

Not so easy. She swallowed hard. 'Yes, all right.
When?'

'Tomorrow? My place?'

She nodded. Twenty-four hours. All the time in the
world. Except when you were making the most important decision of your life.

And it didn't get any easier. Lying awake that night,
tossing and turning, watching the hands of the clock drag
their way round, she went over and over the arguments
until her head ached.

She tried to be rational, putting aside any personal
feelings. On a purely professional basis she was confi-
dent she could do the job, and Gramps must have
thought so, too, or he wouldn't have made the offer. So
what was the problem?

Kate sighed. The problem was that whichever way she
looked at it, she was the loser. If she stayed it would
mean seeing Nick every day, working with him, knowing that he still loved Christina. On the other hand, if

she were to leave, there were people she would miss. Huw and Megan, the new baby, Ellie.

'Damn it,' she muttered. 'At least be honest with yourself. You want to stay.' But what did Nick want? Groaning, she punched her pillow and dragged the duvet over her head.

Twelve hours later her decision had been made. By the end of the day her head ached and the doubts had come flooding in again. Which didn't bode well for the evening.

Later, having showered and brushed her hair until it shone, Kate studied the contents of her wardrobe and felt the nervousness she had been fighting all day well up again. It had been a mistake ever to agree to have dinner with Nick, especially dinner alone at his house. Far better, far safer, if it had been somewhere neutral. But it was too late to do anything about it now.

She decided finally to wear a trouser suit in black, softly draped fabric, teamed with a silk camisole. Small gold earrings and a matching chain at her throat added a touch of glitter.

She was applying touches of eye shadow when the phone rang. Her heart gave an illogical thud. Could it be Nick, cancelling for some reason? Kate was totally unprepared for the sense of disappointment that washed over her as she snatched up the receiver.

She felt almost relieved when an unfamiliar voice said jerkily, 'Dr Jameson? This is Dan Saunders, from Twin Oaks Farm. I'm sorry to call you out, but we have an emergency over here. A light aircraft has come down in one of my fields. It landed with a hell of a bang. I called the surgery and the answering machine said you were the duty doctor.'

'Yes, that's right.' Kate's response was instantly all

professional. 'Can you give me any details, Mr Saunders?'

'Not a great deal.' He sounded breathless. 'I was out in the yard when I heard the plane overhead. I thought it sounded a bit odd. I could hear the engine spluttering and I guessed he was in trouble. He came down a couple of minutes later. Hit the hedge and ploughed into the field.'

'Do you know how many people were on board?'

'Haven't a clue, sorry. I thought I'd better get help.'

Kate was already reaching for her bag. 'Look, I'm on my way, Dan. Have you alerted the emergency services?'

'They're on their way, but I thought, being the closest, you might be able to get here faster.'

'I'll be with you as soon as I can.' Kate replaced the phone then, after a moment's hesitation, picked it up again and dialled. She felt her heart thud as Nick answered, sounding so close that she wished she could reach out and touch him. There was a note of tension in his voice.

'Kate? What's wrong? You're not going to chicken out on me, are you?'

'Not exactly.' She glanced at her watch. 'Look, I'm sorry but I'm going to be a bit late. I've just had a call. If you'd rather cancel—'

'What's the problem?' he asked sharply.

'I've just had Dan Saunders on the phone. A small plane has come down in one of his fields. I need to get over there as fast as I can, but I thought I'd better let you know, just in case you wanted—'

'I don't see any reason to cancel,' he said. 'We'll still both need to eat. It doesn't matter what time. Look, the meal can be put on hold. Give me some details and I'll meet you at the scene. It could be nasty.'

Kate stiffened. 'There's no need. I'm duty doctor. I'll take care of it. Besides…' she forced a laugh '…you don't get out of doing the cooking that easily.'

'Kate—'

'Sorry, I have to go.' She slammed the phone down quickly, before she was tempted to change her mind, and ran out to the car.

It took ten minutes, driving at what, at any other time, she would have regarded as recklessly on the narrow country roads to the farm.

Pulling into the yard, she grabbed her bag and ran through the rain towards the man who came to meet her.

'Mr Saunders,' she said breathlessly. 'I'm Dr Jameson. You called me.'

He nodded, directing a flashlight so that she could pick her way across the yard. 'Thanks for getting here so quickly, Doc. It's over this way. The police got here a couple of minutes ago. The fire brigade and ambulance are on their way.'

'How bad is it?'

'Looks pretty bad to me.' He held open a gate for her to pass through. 'It landed with one hell of a thump. I'm only surprised the whole thing hasn't gone up in flames. Here, watch your step.'

She flung out a hand as her foot twisted on the rutted ground as they picked their way across the field towards the wreckage.

'It's over there, by those trees.'

Kate drew a deep breath and coughed, covering her nose and mouth with her gloved hand. 'My God, what is that?'

'Aviation fuel. The tank must have ruptured when it

hit the ground. The stuff's leaking all over the place. That's why I couldn't get too close. Sergeant?'

Dan Saunders led her towards the police officer. 'This is Dr Jameson.'

'Doctor. I'm Gordon Mills. Glad to see you. We only just got here. It's risky getting too close. The whole thing could go up any minute, but we've had a quick look.'

Kate gasped with horror at the impacted wreckage of the small plane. 'Have you managed to locate the pilot?'

He nodded grimly. 'It looks as if he took the full impact. It's not a pretty sight. I shouldn't think he stood a chance.'

'I have to take a look anyway. Perhaps you'd better move everyone else away. Is there any sign of the fire brigade?'

'They're on their way.'

'Well, we can't wait. If there's any chance of anyone being alive in there, we want them out, fast.'

'You're taking a hell of a risk, Doc.'

'It's my job.' Kate flashed him a wry smile. 'I'm going to need some light.'

'I'm coming with you.' Dan was already edging his way towards the plane.

She flung him a look. 'You don't have to do this. There's no reason why you should put yourself at risk.'

'I want to. Besides, you'll need some help to move him.'

'Let's find out first if he *can* be moved. I'll have to make an examination before I can judge.'

'You may not have much choice, Doc.'

She looked at him and dashed the rain from her face as she leaned a hand against the wreckage, steadying herself as she peered into what was left of the small cockpit. 'Shine the light in here, can you?' She grunted as her foot slipped and she had to adjust her foothold in order to peer inside.

'Can you see him?'

She nodded. 'You're right. It doesn't look good. I need my stethoscope. It's in my bag.'

'I'll get it.' Sergeant Mills was close behind them. 'I thought you might need some more help.' He snapped the locks on her bag and handed her the stethoscope before directing the light from his own torch into the cockpit. 'Jeez!'

'I can't…reach.' Carefully, Kate eased her head and shoulders into the confined space, wincing as a fragment of the shattered cockpit caught her arm. 'It's…all right. He's slumped over, but I've got him.'

She gritted her teeth. 'Can you get the light any closer? Yes, that's fine. Hold it there.' Her foot slipped again and she cursed softly under her breath. The rain was, if anything, coming down even more heavily, and her fingers were numb as she pressed them against the man's neck. Her heart lurched. 'He's still alive. I've got a pulse.'

'You're kidding.'

Somewhere in the background Kate heard the sound of the ambulance.

'It's very faint, but it's there.' She eased the man's jacket aside, applying her stethoscope to his chest. For the first time she saw his features clearly. His dark hair was matted with blood. He was about forty, she guessed.

He moaned softly.

'Don't try to move,' she cautioned. 'I'm a doctor. You've had an accident but we're going to get you out of here. I just need to check you over first, before we try to move you.'

There was a sudden movement behind her. A hand

touched her arm. 'Dr Jameson? Tony Walker, para-medic. What can I do to help?'

She half turned her head to glance at him and said softly, 'He's still alive but he's in a bad way. We're going to have to cut him free.'

'The fire brigade are here now.'

Kate gave a small sigh of relief. 'We'll have to work on the assumption that he has internal injuries. I'm just checking him over now.'

'Do we know his name?'

'It's Perry Vincent,' Sergeant Mills said. 'Local businessman. He often flies from the local airfield over to Europe.'

The man moaned again.

'All right, Perry,' Kate murmured reassuringly. 'Can you tell me where the pain is?' Her fingers made a gentle examination. A few minutes later she turned to Tony Walker. 'He's got a fracture of the right arm. I can see the bone. I'm guessing he's got several broken ribs, head injuries. Spinal injuries are a possibility, although he says he can feel his legs. If you can pass me a line I'll get the painkiller into him, then you can think about moving him.'

Somehow, in the darkness, people had converged on the scene, and it was almost a relief to be able to stand back and let the emergency services take over.

Half an hour later, Kate picked her way unsteadily to where the chief fire officer was talking to Gordon Mills.

'How's he doing, Doc?'

'I'll be a damn sight happier when he's on his way to hospital.' She drew a deep breath and gave a shaky laugh. 'He's lucky to be alive. I wouldn't have given much for his chances.'

'I'd say it's a miracle he managed to put the plane

down at all. I suppose it could have been worse. He missed the farmhouse by about a hundred yards. In which case we could have been dealing with a lot more casualties.'

'This one isn't out of the woods yet,' Kate reminded them.

'Maybe not, but he's got a better chance than he would have if you hadn't got here so quickly.'

Gordon Mills glanced up at the sky. 'The emergency helicopter rescue service boys are on their way.'

'I'd better go and check on my lads. Another couple of minutes and we should have him out of there and on his way to hospital.'

It was another half an hour before Kate finally made her way slowly back to her car and sat for several minutes gazing back at the scene, before starting up the engine and driving to Nick's.

Nick opened the door as her car pulled up on the drive. He came out to meet her, put his arm around her and led her into the house.

'I was beginning to think you weren't going to make it.'

She gave a slight laugh. 'I wasn't so sure myself there for a while.'

'You need a drink.' His eyes were dark as he looked at her. 'Here.' He poured a large brandy, handing her the glass. 'Drink this. It will do you good.'

She wasn't so sure about that! On an empty stomach it was likely to have the opposite effect. 'I'm not so sure this is a good idea.'

'It's purely medicinal.' He gave a wry smile. 'Trust me, I'm a doctor. It'll do you good.'

She sipped at the golden liquid and closed her eyes briefly, relishing its warmth as it slid down her throat.

'Do you want to tell me about it?'

'There's not much to tell.'

'Kate, there was a report about the crash on the local TV news. You didn't mention anything about a fuel leak.'

'I didn't learn about until after I'd called you.' She frowned, wondering why he was so angry. There was something disturbingly arousing about him as he stood with the firelight behind him, dark trousers hugging his hips, his jaw rigid with tension. 'I suppose I didn't have time to think about the possibility of a fuel leak. It was a job, that's all.' She took another sip at her brandy, only to have the glass removed firmly from her grasp as Nick looked at her for a long moment before pulling her roughly towards him.

'I can't believe you're saying that. I've been going through all kinds of hell here, waiting for news, knowing the kind of risks you were taking. Suppose the damn thing had gone up in flames.'

'But it didn't.' His anger confused her. It seemed to imply a feeling she knew didn't exist. Colour darkened her cheeks. 'Nick, I don't understand what you're trying to say. Or are you implying that I'm not capable of doing my job?'

'No.'

'Then what?' Anger flared. Why was she letting this happen? It seemed she only had to be near him for her emotions to run riot. It left her confused and emotionally drained when what she needed more than anything right now was to be able to think clearly. 'I was doing what I was trained to do, Nick. If that means sometimes taking risks, well, so be it. It's all a part of it.'

He drew a harsh breath. 'And what if I say I don't want you taking those risks?

'Well, then, that's tough, Nick.' She faced him, breathing hard. Suddenly it hit her that they were arguing and she couldn't understand why. Fighting with Nick was the last thing she wanted. She was tired. She had done what she could for Perry Vincent, but there were no guarantees he would make it, and she still had to make decisions about her future. This wasn't turning out to be the kind of evening she had planned and, right now, it was all too much.

For a brief moment, as tears welled up, she closed her eyes, only to open them again as his hands tightened on her arms.

'Damn it, Kate,' he ground out, 'don't you understand what I'm trying to say? I don't want to have to live with the fear, each time you go out, that I might not see you again.' He drew a ragged breath. 'I don't want to lose you. God knows, I hadn't planned on this happening.'

She swallowed hard. 'I...I don't understand. You'll have to explain.'

'I'm saying...' He gave a harsh laugh, then reached out a hand to touch her cheek, the full softness of her mouth. The effect was more potent even than the brandy. She shivered in spite of the heat suddenly burning in her cheeks and tried to turn away.

His own breathing was ragged as he held her, turning her roughly back towards him. His face was drawn into a frown and she could sense the tension in him as his hand cupped her chin, forcing her to look into the compelling blue eyes.

'Kate, I want you.' His shuddering breath whispered against her throat, against her lips, hair and back to her mouth, then his lips claimed hers with a fierce possession that left them both breathless.

She responded with a ferocity that matched his own.

His hands were warm against the silkiness of her skin and he groaned. 'I lose control whenever I'm near you. Have you any idea how much I need you?' he breathed. 'How much I want you to be part of my life?'

Kate stared at him, feeling her breath snag in her throat. 'I want you, too. I thought it must be obvious.' She broke off with a moan as he kissed her again.

His hands moved, tracing the full, soft curves of her breasts. A deep groan rose from his throat. His arms tightened round her as if he was afraid she might slip away.

The sensations he was creating seemed to flood through her, setting off a train of tiny explosions, offering promises but never bringing the fulfilment she craved.

She could feel the heat of his body through the sweatshirt he was wearing, heard her own tiny cry of protest as it seemed to create a barrier between them. Her hands moved jerkily in an attempt to remove it, finally making contact with the smooth silkiness of his skin. 'Oh, Nick, I love you,' she whispered.

Kate felt him tense and wanted to weep as his mouth freed hers. She wasn't even aware of having spoken the words aloud until he looked down at her, his breathing uneven, his eyes narrowed.

'I didn't intend for this to happen,' he ground out.

She looked at him in silence for a moment. 'I…I don't understand. Are you saying you…you didn't intend making love to me?'

'You must know I'd never have any regrets about that.'

'Then what…?' She stared at him, holding her breath until dull realisation began to dawn. 'It's Christina, isn't it?' she murmured thickly. 'Yes, of course. How could

I have thought…?' She saw him frown, then he drew her roughly towards him when she would have pulled away.

'What are you saying? Christina has nothing to do with any of this.'

'No?' Kate sighed. 'I think you're fooling yourself, Nick. Let's just leave it, shall we? This isn't getting us anywhere.'

'We can't just leave it.'

'We don't have any choice,' she said dully. 'She'll always be there, won't she, Nick? It's all right, I understand how you still feel about her. No one could ever take her place.'

He stared at her. 'Kate, this doesn't make sense. Do you honestly believe I could feel as I do, respond as I do, if I still loved Christina?'

'I don't know,' she said flatly. 'I suppose it's possible.'

'Not for me.'

'Then why?' She drew a deep breath and saw him frown.

'This isn't just about Christina. She walked out of my life, yes, but it didn't end there. It *couldn't* end there, don't you see?'

Kate swallowed hard. 'You mean because of Ellie?'

His expression was brooding, his eyes very dark. 'Ellie is part of me, part of my life. She always will be. Nothing's going to change that.'

'I don't see why it has to be a problem.'

His mouth was tight as he looked at her, then he drew her slowly towards him. 'I wish it was as simple as you make it sound.'

'But isn't it?'

He frowned. 'I want you, Kate, but don't you see?

I'm not free. How could I expect anyone to take on a ready-made family?'

Kate gave a slight laugh as her hands pushed gently against the taut, muscular warmth of his chest. 'Has it never occurred to you, Nick, that the problem may not exist except in your own mind?'

His thumb grazed gently against her cheek. 'I'd like to believe that,' he said softly.

'Try very hard.'

'Right now I think I just want to kiss you.'

She sighed, fretfully, when Nick raised his head to look down at her.

'I think we'd better eat,' he murmured huskily, 'before I forget the real reason why you're here. Besides, there is a limit to my powers of self-control.' He sobered then. 'I don't want to rush things, Kate. We've all the time in the world so let's just eat, shall we?'

She told herself she wouldn't be able to eat a thing, but when it came to it she demolished the lightly poached salmon and salad. Nick poured white wine.

'One glass won't do any harm.'

Her head was already spinning, though not entirely from the effects of the alcohol.

'That was marvellous. I must have been more hungry than I realised,' she confessed shamefacedly. 'And you've hardly touched yours.'

Nick grinned, pouring more wine. 'Oh, I had far more interesting things on my mind.'

He stood behind her chair, bending close to fill her glass, and she could smell the subtle tones of his after-shave. His nearness was creating an intensity of sexual awareness she had never known before.

'Tell me about it,' she murmured.

'I think I can do better than that,' he said huskily.

'Let's drink a toast,' he raised his glass. 'To the future—
*our* future.'

Kate sipped at her glass, then set it down. 'Mmm,
that's heady stuff. I can't think straight.'

'Are you sure it's the alcohol?'

She wasn't sure. How could she be when he had this
sort of effect on her?

Nick drew her to her feet, held her within the warm
circle of his arms. 'I'll make coffee later. Right now we
have a lot of talking to do. Besides, I'm not at all sure
I can bear to let you go.' His hands were moving over
her body, rousing her again.

She closed her eyes. 'I'm not sure this is a good idea,'
she murmured breathlessly, tilting her head back to look
at him. 'It's getting late. I need some sleep if I'm going
to turn up at the surgery in any sort of fit state in the
morning.'

His warm breath was against her hair. 'We're going
to have to talk to Alec, you do realise that?'

'Alec?' she murmured breathlessly.

A nerve pulsed in his jaw, then he groaned softly as
his mouth made teasing advances against her lips, her
throat, the lobes of her ears and back to her unresisting
mouth, claiming it with a ferocity that left them both
breathless.

'I think we should let him know as soon as possible
that you'll be staying on, don't you?'

She groaned, pushing him away slightly as he nibbled
at her ear.

'I hadn't actually made my decision,' she said weakly.

'Then perhaps I can help you.' Nick's fingers had long
since dealt with the tiny buttons of her camisole and
were moving over her body, rousing her to a peak of
desperation. 'You're a good doctor, Kate. You're needed

in Felldale, and at least I shall know I can stop worrying about you.'

She closed her eyes, moaning softly as a whole gamut of emotions ran through her. Her senses still felt drugged as she looked up at him. 'You don't have any reason to worry about me.'

'I want to be sure of that.' He raised his head to look down at her with glittering eyes. 'I don't ever want to go through the kind of hell I went through tonight, waiting, wondering what was happening, not even sure I'd ever see you again.'

Kate tried to dismiss the sudden qualm that rippled through her, but it wasn't that easy as a tiny alarm bell started to ring somewhere in her head, so faintly that she hardly registered it. 'I told you, Nick, I was doing my job. It goes with the territory.'

'But it needn't. It doesn't have to.'

Involuntarily she stiffened. 'So, are you saying it's all right for you to take risks, but not for me? Is that it?' She frowned. 'Are you telling me I should stick to working at the surgery and worrying about you?'

'Why not?'

'Because it won't work.' Kate tensed, waiting for his response. A tiny ripple of panic was building inside her. Why did she suddenly feel a gulf opening up between them?

A spasm flickered briefly across his features. 'I thought it was what we both wanted.'

'You assumed it was what I wanted,' she said flatly, detaching herself slowly from his arms. 'You can't make all the rules, Nick. Partnerships don't work that way. They're all about respecting each other's individuality as well as needs, and my needs don't change just because they don't happen to suit you.'

'Kate, you're making too much of this.'

'No,' she said flatly, 'I don't think so. It's important we understand each other now.' Colour heightened her cheeks. 'More to the point, what makes you think you have the right to make decisions for me where my work is concerned?'

'I thought you'd given me that right, the right to love you,' he rasped harshly. 'Obviously I was mistaken.'

'Maybe we both were.' She stared at him. He had mentioned want and need. He hadn't, she realised now, mentioned love or marriage.

Nick frowned. 'Are you saying it's wrong of me not to want you to take risks?' he demanded. 'I don't think I can do that.'

But wasn't he asking her to take the biggest risk of all? He wanted a relationship without the ultimate commitment. He might tell himself he no longer loved Christina, but how could she be sure?

Kate turned away and reached for her jacket. 'I'm sorry. This was a mistake.'

'Kate, please—'

'It's late. I have to go.' She was already moving towards the door. 'I think from now on it would be better if we stick to a strictly business relationship. That way no one gets hurt.'

But it was already too late as far as she was concerned. Maybe, if she could accept Nick on his terms... But she knew now that she couldn't. For her there could be no half-measures. Loving Nick, she wanted...needed...a total commitment in return, and that, it seemed, was the one thing he wasn't prepared to give.

# CHAPTER TEN

WHEN she climbed into bed later, Kate's numbed senses were gradually lulled into an exhausted sleep, to be punctuated by dreams in which someone was ringing a bell. Except that it wasn't a dream. When finally she stirred and pushed aside the duvet to peer at the clock, it was to the horrifying realisation that the alarm had rung itself to a standstill. Consequently she arrived at the surgery ten minutes late, breathless, and with a splitting headache.

Any hopes she might have had of avoiding Nick were instantly dashed as he appeared just as she was at the reception desk, making her apologies to Annie and the waiting patients.

For an instant their eyes met and she experienced a brief sense of shock. He looked as if he had scarcely slept. More than that, he looked drained. His mouth was tight, his blue eyes hard.

'Remind me to sign that insurance form for Mr Latimer, will you?' Kate said to Annie, before turning away deliberately to study her list of calls with an attention it didn't warrant.

'Kate, wait.' Nick's hand came down on her arm. 'Can you spare a minute? I need to talk to you.'

'I'm sorry, I can't. I'm busy. I don't have time.' She tried to sidestep him but he was blocking her path, his face taut as he looked at her.

'We can't just walk away, Kate, as if what happened doesn't matter. It's important.'

'Nothing's changed, Nick.' And besides, what was there to say? The only thing she was certain of was that she felt the distance between them as painfully as if it were a tangible thing.

She had tried to ignore it, but that wasn't easy, not when she'd found herself awake in the early hours and the doubts had come crowding in. What if she had made a mistake? Was he going through the same kind of anguish, the soul-searching?

She gave him a remote smile and turned away. 'I don't seem to have Mrs Stevens's notes. If you could rustle them up for me, Annie? I thought I'd pop in and see her later.'

Annie's glance flickered between the two of them. 'I'll go and get them for you now.'

'Thanks. I'll make a start, then. At this rate I'll be lucky to get back from my calls before afternoon surgery.'

She started to make her way along the corridor. Nick followed, his expression grim. 'Kate, please… Have you spoken to Alec yet?'

'No.' She hesitated in the doorway. Her emotions were so close to the surface that she wasn't sure she could trust herself to be near him without letting go. 'I thought I'd call him later.' Before she had a chance to change her mind.

'Can't we at least talk?'

'It won't make any difference,' she said flatly. 'We did our talking last night. I won't change my mind. The sooner I leave Felldale, the better. That way we can both get on with our lives.'

'But it doesn't have to be—'

'Oh, Nick, there's a call for you.' Jill's voice broke into the tension between them.

'Damn it, can't you take a message?'

'It's Mrs Duncan. She's worried about her husband. She says he seems very breathless. I thought you'd prefer to deal with it.'

He swore softly under his breath. 'I'm on my way. Kate, please…'

But she was already walking away. If she talked to Nick, she would end up in his arms. Cowardice was the only defence she had left, and she was clinging to it as if her life depended on it.

Somehow she got through the morning. 'See how you get on with the tablets, Mrs Graham. They're fairly new and I've had good reports on them, but if you don't feel better in a few days, come back and we'll try you on something else.' She escorted her patient to the door. 'And try to rest.' She smiled. 'I know it isn't easy, but that leg needs time to heal. You're not doing yourself any favours by trying to soldier on.'

Returning to her room, she made a phone call, checked her diary and then made her way to Reception. 'Right, I'm off.' Handing over the cards, she glanced at her watch. 'If I hurry I might even manage to grab a quick cup of coffee before I start my calls.'

Jill glanced anxiously out of the window. 'I was hoping to do a bit of shopping, but from the look of that sky we could be in for some snow.' She pulled a wry face. 'I think I might leave it. It wasn't urgent anyway.'

A door along the corridor opened and Nick emerged, grim-faced.

'Yes, well, I think I'll skip the coffee after all. I'll see you later.' By the time Kate had reached her car and was fumbling to get the key in the lock, Nick was beside her.

She cursed as the key refused to turn. Nick's hand came down over hers. 'I'm not just going to let you walk out of my life, Kate. I don't give in that easily. There must be some way—'

'Nick, please, don't do this.' She kneaded a hand briefly at her aching head. 'There's nothing to talk about. We said everything there was to say.' From the moment Nick Forrester had walked into her life it had become full of complications. Right now she felt as if she were walking on quicksand. The more she struggled to break free, it seemed, the deeper she was being sucked in.

'I can't let you go, not like this.'

'You don't have any choice. It's my decision. No, please, I'm already late.' There was no mistaking the strain on his face. Never before had she been so aware of her own vulnerability where he was concerned. It would be so easy to give in, but then what? Could she really spend the rest of her life living constantly in the shadow of the woman he had loved?

With an effort she turned the key in the lock. 'I'll stay until you can find someone to take my place at the practice. I'm sure you won't have any difficulty.'

His mouth tightened. 'Are you saying that what happened between us meant nothing? That I misread the signals?'

'Maybe we both did.' Heightened colour came into her cheeks as she wrenched open the car door and climbed in. 'I can't be what you want, Nick. I'm not even sure you *know* what you want.'

'I want *you*.'

She sighed and wound down the window. 'I meant what I said, Nick. We'd better keep things to a strictly business relationship. That way neither of us gets hurt.'

But it was already too late for that, she thought as she drove away. The damage, as far as she was concerned, was already done.

Back at the cottage, she made herself a quick cup of coffee before running upstairs to change out of her skirt into a pair of black trousers and a sweater. Having checked the messages on her answering machine, she added one more call to the list before making her way through a heavy downpour of rain towards the car.

By mid-afternoon the rain had turned to snow and she had to switch on the headlights as the light began to fade.

Climbing out of the car at her next port of the call, she locked the door and made a dash across the farm-yard. The door was opened by an anxious-looking Betty Jarvis.

'I'm sorry it's taken me a while to get to you, Betty,' Kate apologised as she stepped into the large, flagstone-floored kitchen, brushing flakes of snow from her hair as she did so. 'This weather is making the roads quite icy.'

'Aye, and I reckon we'll get a lot more of this before the winter's out. Will you have a cup of tea, Doctor? Warm you up a bit. I was just about to take one up to Dad.'

'I'm tempted, Betty.' Kate glanced, frowning, at her watch. 'But I'd better not. I've still a few more calls to make and I'd like to get back to the surgery before dark if possible.'

'Fair enough. Perhaps you'll take a few fresh eggs with you when you go?'

Kate smiled. 'That would be lovely.'

She liked Betty Jarvis. She had the weathered features of someone who had always lived and worked on the land. Her father had been a farmer and she had married a farmer. Following her husband's death in an accident some years ago, her son had helped out, but Kate knew that things hadn't been easy for the close-knit family, especially when her elderly father had had a stroke and needed looking after.

'How is your dad, Betty?'

'Not so good this past couple of days.' Shedding her apron, Betty led the way towards the stairs. 'He had a bit of a cold last week. It didn't seem too bad, more of a snuffle really. I thought he was getting over it, but he's started coughing.'

'You should have called me.'

'Well, you know what he's like. Anything upsets his routine and he gets flustered, but when he decided to stay in bed I knew it was more serious.' She pushed open the door. 'Dad, it's Dr Jameson come to see you. You remember the doctor, don't you?'

'Hello, Stan, how are you? Betty tells me you've not been feeling too well.'

The occupant of the bed raised one frail hand, turning his head to look in Kate's direction.

'I'd like to listen to your chest, if that's all right? Have you got any pain anywhere?'

With Betty supporting her father, Kate made a gentle but thorough examination before removing her stethoscope and helping to lay him gently back against the pillows.

She smiled. 'All right, Stan, I won't bother you any more. You try to rest.' Moving slightly away from the bed, she said, 'He's got a bit of a chest infection bubbling away in there.'

'Oh, no. I was afraid you might say that. So, what do we do?'

'Well, ideally, I'd like to get him into hospital for a few days.'

'He's not going to like that.'

'No, I realise that. The trouble is, he's much less mobile than he was before he had the stroke, and I really think, for a few days at least, he needs hospital care where the experts can keep an eye on him.'

'I know it makes sense.' Betty's face was troubled. 'Convincing him is going to be the problem. I'd better have a chat with him, explain what's happening, or he'll only get himself into a state.'

'I'll phone for an ambulance,' Kate said. 'It'll take them a while to get here so you'll have time to pack a few necessities, toiletries, that sort of thing. And try not to worry, Betty. It really is for the best and I'm sure they'll soon having him feeling much better.'

It was dark by the time Kate finally managed to finish her calls and return to the practice. She parked her car and ran, head bowed against the buffeting wind, into the surgery.

A quick peep into the crowded waiting room and the expectant looks on the faces turned in her direction sent her hurrying through to Reception.

'What on earth's going on? Where's Nick, for heaven's sake? He can't have forgotten it's evening surgery.'

'We haven't heard from him.'

The phone rang. Frowning, Jill reached for it, cupping her hand over the receiver. 'He did have quite a few calls. I expect they're taking a bit longer than he expected. I'm sure he'll be here soon.'

'Well, I hope so. It's like rush hour at Waterloo station out there.'

'It's not like him to be late, especially when he said he expected to be back on time.'

'Have you tried to reach him on his mobile?'

'Yes. He's not answering.'

A tiny and thoroughly illogical finger of fear stabbed at Kate's heart. What if something had happened? An accident? The roads were pretty treacherous and it was snowing.

Mentally she shook herself. This was ridiculous. There was probably some perfectly logical reason why he was late.

With an effort she fought to bring her feelings under control. 'Well, look, I'll make a start,' she said briskly. 'But at this rate I could be here all night. In the meantime, keep trying to reach Nick.' She gave a mock groan as a pile of cards was thrust into her hands. 'You're sure you couldn't find a few more?'

'Probably. If you're very lucky.' Jill grinned.

Kate fled to her consulting room where she shed her jacket, glancing briefly out of the window. It was snowing even harder now. Where are you, Nick? she thought. Suddenly she found herself wishing he would call. Better still, that he would walk through the door, that he would be here, touchable, safe.

For the next two hours she worked steadily, sighing with relief as, finally, she saw her last patient to the door. 'Now that we've had the test results back, Mrs Hayward, and we know what we're dealing with, I'm sure you'll find the antibiotics will do the trick.'

'Well, I can't say I'll be sorry about that. This damned infection seems to have been going on for ever.'

Smiling, Kate followed her along the corridor. Nick's door was closed. A peep into the waiting room showed it to be still crowded. He wasn't back, then. Alarm bells started ringing inside her head as she made her way to the office.

'What's happening? Is there still no sign of Nick?'

'Not so far.'

Instinctively Kate's glance went to the clock. 'But…' She felt the blood draining from her face. 'Surely he can't have forgotten the time? He knows it's evening surgery.'

'I've had a word with the patients,' Annie interjected quietly. 'Most of them are happy to come back tomorrow, but a few decided to hang on, just in case.'

'Right.' Kate was finding it hard to concentrate. 'But what's happened to Nick? If there's a problem he should have rung in by now.'

'We've been trying to contact him but he's still not answering his mobile.'

'Kate.' Jill was holding the phone. Frowning, she looked at Kate and held out the receiver. 'I think you'd better take this.'

Kate shook her head. 'Not now.' She couldn't think.

'I think you should,' Jill said quietly. 'It's Ellie.'

'Ellie?' Kate turned slowly to face the other woman, her fear becoming tangible, something to be held off as long as she didn't give a name to it. She swallowed hard on the sudden dryness in her throat. 'You mean…Nick and Ellie.'

Jill shook her head and Kate felt her stomach tighten. 'I've been phoning around, trying to contact Nick. As a last resort I tried ringing him at home. I didn't think anyone was going to answer, then…' she bit at her lower lip '…Ellie picked up the phone.'

Kate felt as if everything was suddenly moving in slow motion. She reached out to take the phone.

'Hello, Ellie?' With an effort she managed to keep her voice even. 'This is Kate.'

There was a muffled sound, as if the child was holding the phone close to her mouth. 'Kate?'

'Yes, hello, poppet. How are you?'

There was a brief pause and a rustling sound. 'I'm fine.'

Kate drew a steadying breath. 'Have your spots all gone?'

'Yes. Daddy kissed them better.'

Oh, lucky Ellie. Kate closed her eyes briefly, forcing herself to concentrate. 'Ellie, is Daddy there?'

'Yes.'

'Ellie…?'

'I climbed on the chair and answered the phone all by myself.'

'You…you climbed on the chair to answer the phone?' Kate glanced at Jill who moved suddenly closer, her hand fluttering nervously to her throat. 'Ellie, where is Daddy?'

There was a pause during which she could hear rustling sounds, as if small hands were juggling with the phone. Please, please, don't drop it. Kate moistened her dry lips with her tongue. 'Ellie?'

'Daddy's asleep.'

'Asleep?' Nick asleep while his daughter was in the house? Kate was vaguely aware of Annie reaching out a hand.

'Yes. He was going to make me some chips and some fish fingers, but he falled asleep.'

Kate drew a ragged breath and said softly, 'She says Nick is asleep.'

'Oh, God.'

'Ellie?' Kate cleared her throat. 'How long has Daddy been asleep?'

Again there was a muffled rustling sound.

'Ellie?' Panic edged Kate's voice.

'He's beened asleep a long time. Kate?'

'Yes, sweetheart.'

'I'm hungry.'

'Are you, sweetheart?' Kate's hands were suddenly shaking. 'Ellie, have you tried to wake Daddy?'

'Yes, but he won't wake up.' Something closely akin to a small sob touched the child's voice. 'I 'spect he didn't have his 'jection.'

Kate closed her eyes and leaned heavily on the reception desk. 'Ellie, where is Daddy?'

'He's on the floor.'

'Where, sweetheart?' Her heart was thudding so hard now she felt as if it would burst. 'Which floor, Ellie? Can you see him?'

'Yes.'

Kate cupped her hand briefly over the receiver. 'She says Nick's on the floor, in the living room, asleep.'

Jill's face drained of colour. She said softly, 'Hypo-glycaemia?'

'It could be. The question is, how long…?'

'Kate?'

'Yes, Ellie. I'm here, sweetheart.'

'Scwuffy is very fwightened.'

Kate's heart lurched. 'Is he, poppet? Well, look, he musn't be frightened because everything is going to be all right.' She glanced at Jill. 'Ellie, I want you to do something for me, sweetheart. I want you to give Scruffy a big cuddle and you tell him that I'm going to come and see you, right now. Tell him I'll be there in about…five minutes.' And, please, God, it wouldn't be too late. 'I'm going to put the phone down now, Ellie, and I'm going out to my car.' She was talking to herself. Ellie had already replaced the receiver.

Kate was already reaching for her bag. She glanced up at Sue, who had obviously been listening. 'Sue, I'll need you to come with me. Someone will have to look after Ellie while I see to Nick.'

'I'm with you.'

Together they ran out to the car. Kate wasn't even aware of driving to the house. She pulled up on the drive, grabbed her bag and ran to the door at the rear of the house.

Ellie was sitting on the stairs with Scruffy. Her small face was flushed and tear-stained. 'Kate, I knewed you would come. I told Scwuffy.'

Kate hugged her. 'You're very brave and I love you both.' She looked at Sue and smiled. 'This is Sue. She's come with me to see Daddy.' She nodded in the direction of the sitting room. 'It's through here.' Please, God, we're in time.

Nick was lying on the floor. His face was ashen, he was obviously deeply unconscious.

Kate fell to her knees beside him, feeling for a pulse. Her eyes blurred with sudden tears. 'He's alive. I need to do a finger-prick test.'

'Here. Can you manage?'

'I'll be fine. Can you prepare an injection of glucose solution?' Kate briefly clenched her trembling hands. 'Come on, *come on.*' Somehow she managed to ease a tiny spot of blood onto the test strip and inserted it into the meter. 'The reading is below one,' she said raggedly. 'Let's get that glucose into him, fast. It should bring him round.'

Five minutes later Nick groaned.

'Nick? Can you hear me?' Kate cupped his face in her hands, shaking him gently. 'Nick, come on, wake up. Damn it! Open your eyes.'

He moved his arm, covering his eyes.

'Nick, it's Kate.' She bent closer. 'Your blood sugar

level is too low. You passed out.' She shook him again. 'Come on. Say something.'

He tried to open his eyes. Kate glanced at Sue. 'He's still confused. Check the fridge, see if there's any Coke or a chocolate bar, anything sweet that will help to bring his levels up.'

Ellie ran into the kitchen, opened the fridge and dragged out a bottle of cola.

Sue followed her. 'Clever girl.' Then she found a glass, poured cola into it and took it in to Kate. Kate supported Nick's shoulders and fed the liquid gently between his lips.

He tried to push it away. 'Nick, you have to drink it, all of it.' Somehow, with an effort, she managed to persuade him to empty the glass. 'Good, that's good. I'm going to take another finger-prick test now, just to check your levels again.'

She carried out the second test, checked the reading and gave a sigh of relief. 'It's up to four.'

'Is Daddy better now?'

Kate blinked away a sudden misting of tears. 'Yes, poppet, I think he is. He's going to be fine.'

Sue gave a deep sigh and grinned. 'I think I'll just find this young lady something to eat. I reckon she deserves it, don't you? How about that, Ellie?'

'Scwuffy's hungry, too.'

'I'll bet he is.' Hand in hand, the two of them went into the kitchen to investigate the fridge.

Kate sat on the floor, holding Nick's hand, watching the colour return slowly to his face. His features looked haggard. 'Come back to me, Nick,' she said quietly. She swallowed hard on the lump in her throat. 'What on earth did you think you were doing? Can't I let you out of my sight for five minutes without you doing something crazy?'

His fingers twined slowly with hers and, with an effort, he opened his eyes. Instinctively she squeezed his hand. 'Kate?'

She closed her eyes and blinked hard before giving a forced laugh. 'Well, welcome back.'

'Wh-what happened?' he said huskily.

'You passed out. Your blood sugar level was almost zero. When did you last eat?'

He groaned and flung the back of his hand across his eyes. 'Oh, God. I took my last insulin injection and I remember thinking a while later that I should eat something, then I had another call. I was already running late.' His eyes widened. 'Ellie…?'

'It's all right. She's fine. She's in the kitchen with Sue.'

Nick drew a ragged breath and managed to sit up, resting his back weakly against the cupboard. 'I can vaguely remember driving home. I knew I should eat something but that's the damned thing about diabetes, when you *should* eat, you don't want to. I knew I had to look after Ellie…' He turned his head to look at her. 'I was getting more and more confused. I don't remember anything after that, until I woke up and saw you. But how…?'

Kate gave a shaky smile. 'Jill was phoning round to try to contact you. She eventually tried calling here and Ellie answered. I guessed what must have happened.'

'And you came rushing over?'

'I'm a doctor. It's my job.' She refused to meet his gaze, felt the muscles in his arm tense as he eased himself into a sitting position.

His glittering gaze narrowed as he looked at her. 'Am

I mistaken or did I hear you suggesting that I needed looking after?'

She gave a slight laugh. 'That sounds like a pretty full-time job to me.'

He rose unsteadily to his feet, taking her with him, and for a few seconds she was held within the warm circle of his arms. It was a mistake. His nearness set a mass of ill-timed signals firing in her brain.

Her hand reached up and she was surprised to find that it was shaking. 'You must have cut your head when you fell.' She frowned. 'It needs cleaning up. By rights you should go to hospital for a check-up.' Suddenly her voice had an edge to it. She was angry without really knowing why. She said briskly, 'How do you feel?'

'Like an idiot, and my head aches.'

'Well, what do you expect?' she snapped ungraciously. 'You were damn lucky, Nick. How could you be so stupid? You know how important it is to eat regularly—' She broke off, suddenly shivering violently. Only now was reaction beginning to set in. Taking several deep breaths, she half turned away, only to feel Nick's hands on her shoulders, preventing her.

'Kate, what's wrong?'

She couldn't believe he was asking the question. He could have died and he wanted to know what was wrong! She looked up, her face taut with strain, to find him watching her, his lips set in a hard, fierce line.

'Wrong? Nothing's wrong. Why should anything be wrong?'

His own breathing was ragged as he held her, his hand cupping her chin, forcing her to look into the compelling blue eyes. 'Kate, it's all right.'

'It isn't all right.' Anger gave an edge to her voice. 'Have you any idea what I've been through? You might have been unconscious for hours, for all I knew. You might have died. How could you? How *could* you?'

His face was gaunt as she stared at him, then, with a sob, she launched herself into his arms. 'I thought I'd lost you. I wanted to die, too.'

He was speaking softly as he held her, his own throat tightening in painful spasms. 'Hey, come on. You don't get rid of me that easily. Everything's going to be all right,' his voice rasped.

'But I thought…' Her voice was muffled as he held her close. 'When I saw you lying there I was so scared. I hadn't realised until then just what—'

'Kate, don't!' His fingers brushed against her mouth, silencing the words, then, before she knew what was happening, his mouth came down on hers, relentless, firm, demanding.

They clung together, Kate offering no resistance as his hands moved over her body. He raised his head briefly to look down at her. 'Oh, God, I need you.' His mouth made a teasing foray, driving her to distraction.

She responded with a ferocity that matched his own, filled with a need to be part of him, to hold him, to keep him safe. The glow from the fire enclosed them both in its warm circle. She could feel the heat of his body through the thin sweatshirt he was wearing. His own hands moved jerkily in an attempt to remove her sweater. He swore softly as it seemed to create a barrier between them, until he finally made contact with the warm silkiness of her skin. 'Kate—oh, Kate, I love you,' he rasped. 'These past twenty-four hours have been hell.'

'For me too,' she said brokenly.

Nick gazed wonderingly into her eyes, then, almost hesitantly, enfolded her again in his arms. 'If it's any consolation, I haven't had a second's peace of mind since last night. I can't believe I just let you walk out.'

Kate had to force herself to speak through the tightness in her throat. 'I don't recall it being a case of you *letting* me walk out,' she said shakily. 'I seem to remember it was my decision. One I've…' She swallowed hard. 'If it was possible to put the clock back, I would.' She could feel the pulse hammering in her throat as he held her at arm's length to stare down at her.

'Kate, are you saying what I think you're saying?'

She stared at him, her green eyes wide with confusion. 'I suppose I'm saying that…maybe I've been too busy thinking about my own needs to think about anyone else's,' she said brokenly. 'What it comes down to is that I know now that I'd rather be with you on any terms than without you and Ellie on mine. Can you understand that? Does it make any kind of sense?'

'I think you may need to explain,' he prompted softly, his eyes narrowed and searching.

'I mean, I think I can see now what you've been going through.' She moistened her dry lips with her tongue. 'I realise that you'll always love Christina, that she'll always be part of your life. I know I could never take her place—'

A groan rose in his throat as he silenced her with a kiss, before raising his head to look at her. 'Kate, you're wrong. What gave you the idea that I still love Christina?' he bit out. 'Believe me, whatever there was between us was over long before she decided to leave. In fact, I'm beginning to doubt that I ever did love her.' He frowned. 'Maybe walking out was the best thing she ever did for Ellie and me.'

She stared at him, wanting to believe him, but fear gave an edge to her voice. 'I don't understand.'

His mouth tightened. 'Maybe we both had a different idea of what we wanted from marriage. I'm not saying it was her fault. Christina liked the *idea* of marriage. Marriage to a consultant held an even greater fascination. Unfortunately the novelty soon wore off.' Nick grimaced. 'I hoped Ellie's birth might bring us closer together.'

'But it didn't?'

His mouth twisted. 'Having a child didn't quite fit in with her plans or the kind of life she was beginning to discover a liking for. After a while I stopped blaming myself and simply accepted the fact that it was nothing personal, no major failing on my part, it was simply the way Christina was. Then you walked into my life, and I suddenly realised that what I had felt for Christina may have been sexual attraction, but it was never love.'

Confusion briefly clouded Kate's eyes. 'But…this house? You were obviously reluctant to sell. I thought it held too many memories, *happy* memories.'

He gave a light, humourless laugh. 'I meant it when I said Ellie had been upset enough. That's the only reason the house is important, Kate. I want her to feel secure, to have some kind of stability in her life.' His hand moved against her hair, caressing her cheek. 'When she's older, then I'll be able to explain, in as gentle a way as possible, what happened, why her mother left.'

'Oh, Nick, she's very lucky to have you,' Kate said softly, made drowsy by the warmth of the fire and the joyful knowledge that she was in his arms.

'I'm the lucky one,' he said huskily as he turned her face up to his. 'I'd made up my mind that I didn't need anything else in my life, that work and Ellie were enough. I love my work.'

'So do I.'

His lips moved against hers. 'I realise that, and I know now that I was being selfish when I tried to place restrictions on it. I had no right. No right at all.'

'We all have to come to terms with our own insecurities. It's what partnership is all about, accepting people for what they are.'

His mouth came down on hers, gently at first, then becoming more demanding until they broke apart, breathlessly.

'I love you, Kate. You do know that?'

She drew a long, shaky breath. 'I love you, too.' The words were muffled as he bent his head, his mouth drifting warmly over her cheek.

He cupped her chin, looking down at her tenderly but still with a hint of the anguish he'd been through in his eyes.

'So, you'll be staying in Felldale, then?'

'It sounds good to me.' Kate stared up at him earnestly.

His lips moved against hers. 'Are you sure? Really sure? I know what it meant to you, coming back to Felldale—raking up all the memories…'

'Yes, I'm sure.' Her fingers brushed lightly against his cheek, moved to his lips, silencing the words. 'I loved Paul. I can't pretend I didn't. He'll always be part of my life. But I know now that I have to move on, get on with my life. That's what he would have wanted. I *want* to move on. I love you, Nick. I love Ellie. I need you both in my life.'

He gazed into her eyes then, almost hesitantly, he drew her towards him. 'You realise I'm asking you to take on more than a job? I'm talking about marriage, Kate.'

'That sounds like quite a commitment. I may need time to think about it.'

He made a soft growling sound in his throat as he bent his head to kiss her again. 'Time's up,' he rasped as he broke away.

Kate grinned. 'Well, since you put it so nicely, and after careful consideration…I accept.'

'Oh, Kate, my Kate.' He hugged her tightly. 'Just think…the three of us together.'

She sighed happily as she rested her head against his chest. 'My trouble in triplicate.'

He raised his head to look at her. 'Triplicate?'

'You forgot Scruffy.'

She closed her eyes as he kissed her again, and when she opened them once more, much later, it was to see Sue standing, grinning, in the doorway, with Ellie at her side.

Ellie giggled, pressing one small hand over her mouth. 'Daddy kissed her better.'

Oh, yes, Kate thought as Nick took her with him to sweep Ellie up, laughing, into his arms. Daddy definitely did kiss her better.

Her breath snagged in her throat as he stroked her hair and his mouth brushed her forehead.

'Happy?'

'I think I can live with it,' she sighed stoically, letting her fingers drift idly beneath his sweatshirt.

'Careful, woman,' he growled. 'You don't know what you're letting yourself in for.'

'So show me,' she murmured, her gaze meeting his with glittering anticipation.

**Modern Romance**™
...seduction and
passion guaranteed

**Tender Romance**™
...love affairs that
last a lifetime

**Sensual Romance**™
...sassy, sexy and
seductive

**Sizzling Romance**™
...sultry days and
steamy nights

**Medical Romance**™
...medical drama on
the pulse

**Historical Romance**™
...rich, vivid and
passionate

*29 new titles every month.*

*With all kinds of Romance for
every kind of mood...*

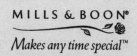

MILLS & BOON®

*Makes any time special*™

MAT3

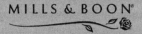

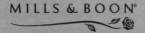

# Medical Romance™

### THE SURGEON'S SECRET *by Lucy Clark*

*Part 2 of the McElroys trilogy*

Dr Alex Page can't risk getting involved with beautiful new research fellow Jordanne McElroy, despite the fact she's everything he's ever wanted in a woman. She is determined to break his resolve, and the closer she gets to his heart, the closer she gets to the secret he's convinced will drive her away.

### MALE MIDWIFE *by Gill Sanderson*

Nursing manager Joy Taylor began to believe she had a future with her unit's only male midwife – even though Chris told her he could never give her a child. But when a million-to-one chance changed everything, instead of sealing their future, it threatened to tear them apart...

### STARRING DR KENNEDY *by Flora Sinclair*

When a tall hunk of a film star shadows Dr Skye Kennedy around the hospital, she's worried about his effect on the patients – and on *her!* Kyle Sullivan had broken her heart before, so how would she ever be able to trust him again?

## On sale 5th October 2001

*Available at most branches of WH Smith, Tesco, Martins, Borders, Easons, Sainsbury, Woolworth and most good paperback bookshops*

0901/03b

# Coming Home

*Scandal drove David away*
*Now love will draw him home . . .*

# PENNY JORDAN

## Published 21st September

# FREE
## 4 BOOKS
### AND A SURPRISE GIFT!

We would like to take this opportunity to thank you for reading this Mills & Boon® book by offering you the chance to take FOUR more specially selected titles from the Medical Romance™ series absolutely FREE! We're also making this offer to introduce you to the benefits of the Reader Service™—

★ FREE home delivery     ★ FREE gifts and competitions
★ FREE monthly Newsletter     ★ Exclusive Reader Service discounts
★ Books available before they're in the shops

Accepting these FREE books and gift places you under no obligation to buy; you may cancel at any time, even after receiving your free shipment. Simply complete your details below and return the entire page to the address below. *You don't even need a stamp!*

**YES!** Please send me 4 free Medical Romance books and a surprise gift. I understand that unless you hear from me, I will receive 6 superb new titles every month for just £2.49 each, postage and packing free. I am under no obligation to purchase any books and may cancel my subscription at any time. The free books and gift will be mine to keep in any case.

M1ZEC

Ms/Mrs/Miss/Mr ..................................................Initials ...........................................
                                                                                          BLOCK CAPITALS PLEASE
Surname .................................................................................................................................
Address ..................................................................................................................................
...............................................................................................................................................
...........................................................Postcode ......................................................

**Send this whole page to:**
**UK: FREEPOST CN81, Croydon, CR9 3WZ**
**EIRE: PO Box 4546, Kilcock, County Kildare (stamp required)**